Out to Get Her

LEIGH LANDRY

OUT TO GET HER by Leigh Landry

Published by Leigh Landry

Lafayette, LA, USA

This is a work of fiction. Names, characters, places, and incidents either are the products of the author's imagination or are used fictitiously.

Chapter One

ERIN HELD up an arm to block the smoke from entering her nostrils. She remembered how people around here liked to burn their trash, but she also remembered the smell of things burning that shouldn't be. Whatever this was, it was definitely in the "shouldn't be burning" camp.

After replacing the gas nozzle, she headed inside the mostly empty station. This place had always been packed every afternoon. Teenagers stopping before and after school for boudin balls and caffeine. Retirees chatting at the counter with nothing better to do on a Wednesday afternoon. And you couldn't get on the lot at lunch when the food was hot out of the fryer and the gossip even hotter.

But for all she knew, this could be the new normal. Maybe half the town had done the smart thing, the same thing Erin had done, and hauled ass right on out of here at the first chance.

The jingle bells rattled from the handle as she entered the building and took a quick left turn toward the coolers. She grabbed two Dr. Peppers, one for later, since the house wouldn't be stocked with anything but orange juice, bread, and deli meats. Then she headed back to the front counter where a tall, dark-bearded man leaned an arm against the hot foods display case while he recounted a recent fishing trip to the cashier. The poor woman's hair was falling out of her ponytail post-lunch-rush, and she looked like she'd heard ten versions of this story already today.

"If it hadn't of been for me, that bastard would of lost that bluegill." The man's voice dripped with arrogance. Although, if Erin could have put money on it, the real story was probably more like "that bastard" having to bail this guy out instead.

She knew the type. They were *all* that type around here. Young. Old. Didn't matter.

The cashier punched in the amount for her drinks as Erin told her which pump she was on. "Who's burning a mattress or whatever out there?"

The woman paused a moment before announcing the total. Then she added, "You didn't hear about Addie's?"

Addie's.

Erin racked her memory for whoever or whatever an Addie was, but she came up short. Best not to admit that, though. The last thing you wanted to be in this town was an outsider. They were probably sizing her up already.

2

Trying to figure out whose kid she was and why they hadn't seen her around lately. Erin just shook her head.

"Didn't you see all that smoke out there behind the building?"

Oh. That Addie's. Addie's Lunch Shack. It was maybe half a football field from this gas station. Had a damn good BLT.

"I could smell it, but couldn't tell where it was coming from."

"They probably put it all out by now, I guess," the woman said. "Grease fire or something."

"That's a shame." Because now Erin had a craving for a BLT, and Adeline Weaver's place was probably still the only "restaurant" in town.

As she handed over her cash, the big man pointed a thick finger at her. "Ain't you Michael's kid?"

Shit.

She was wrong. The absolute last thing you wanted to be in this town was recognized. By anyone. But especially by guys in gas stations who had more time than they knew what to do with.

"Oh, I'm so sorry, honey," the cashier said. "I didn't recognize you. What with the hair and all."

Erin resisted the urge to play with the ends of her wavy turquoise bob and took her change and drinks. "Thanks."

"Your grandpa came in here every weekend for smoked boudin and cracklins. Nicest man around here, I swear. And I'm not just sayin' that."

No irony at all in everyone ignoring the fact that an assumed heart attack had done him in.

Erin nodded in agreement, swallowing the uninvited lump forming in her throat.

Nope. There was absolutely no time for grief. She needed to tamp down this feelings stuff, take care of business, and get the hell back out of this place.

Before she could turn away, that finger pointed at her once again.

"Yeah, I remember you." He squinted hard at her. "When did you get back, girl?"

She struggled to place who this man was so she could deflect the conversation by asking about some cousin of his, but her brain couldn't distinguish him. All the men around here were one big pile of memory mush.

"Just on my way in. Haven't even been to the house yet."

Translation: *Whatever you think I did, it wasn't me.*

This time.

For crying out loud, the one crime she'd actually been investigated for was years ago. How was she going to settle all of her grandpa's affairs and get back to her life if the whole town was still accusing her of every single petty-ass crime. She wouldn't be surprised if someone jumped around the corner and accused her of clogging Grandpa Darryl's artery.

The still-unidentified asshole grunted, and Erin took that as her cue to bail. Once in her car, she twisted open one of the drinks and tossed the other on her passenger seat.

Great, the inside of her car smelled like smoke now. Not that it had smelled delightful before, but at least it hadn't smelled like a grease fire.

She wondered how bad that fire at Addie's really was. Like... was it just a little grease fire that had burned a tiny corner of the kitchen, or was it a no-way-in-hell-you're-getting-a-BLT level of bad?

A peek wouldn't hurt, right?

Curiosity and hunger got the best of her, so she put the cap back on her Dr. Pepper and aimed for the smoke cloud.

"I'm telling you, Sam, someone is out to get me."

Samantha tightened her grip on the pen and clipboard in her hands and fought to unclench her jaw. A stress headache wouldn't do her any good. Especially since this week *and* Addie were out to get Samantha now.

She calmly and silently raised an eyebrow at the late-middle-aged woman before her in the bright pink collared shirt and turquoise apron. Her dark brown hair was tied up in a neat bun, not a strand out of place despite the ruckus of the fire.

"I'm sorry, *Sergeant Ardoin*," she corrected. Her thick Cajun accent oozed through the contempt-laden apology. "But I mean it. And it's *not* post-traumatic stress or whatever. Someone is really out to close my store, I tell you."

This wasn't the first time Adeline Weaver had come up with a wild conspiracy theory, but this was the first one that involved arson. The last thing Samantha needed was a bogus arson complaint a week and a half before the election. Sure, she could clearly prove this was accidental—and had statements to back that up—but the paperwork alone would be a nightmare. Not to mention the hit-job Adeline would initiate if Samantha openly dismissed the woman's crack-pot theory of the week.

"Addie, I just spoke to your own kitchen staff, and they all gave statements that this was an accident."

Three people were on record with the same story. Too many ice crystals on a batch of fries splashed oil onto a nearby burner. Flames went up on the stove, but since Addie kept the hood and grease traps clean, the fire remained pretty isolated. Could have been a lot worse.

"Maybe one of them did it. Or maybe one of them's covering for someone else."

Samantha took a deep breath and tried her best to remain calm. But calm was nearly impossible in this woman's presence. Still, nothing would get solved here today if Samantha lost her cool. Least of all this case.

"So you want to make an official statement suggesting that a member of *your own staff* set fire to your restaurant. Is that what you want me to write down on this piece of paper?"

Addie was a lot of things, many of them not pleasant, but she was by all accounts an excellent person to work for. She treated her employees like family—for good or worse—and bought them each unique gifts every

Christmas and baked them each a cake for their birthdays, all personalized to their tastes.

"Well, no." She frowned. "Aw hell, don't you dare write that down."

Samantha raised her brow, but put the pen down.

"And don't give me that eye, *Sergeant Ardoin*. I changed your diapers for a year when your mama first went back to work. You may be a grown woman now and a sergeant, but I will not have you disrespecting me with those pretty brown eyes of yours."

The diaper thing. Again. It was Addie's one card to play whenever she was in some kind of trouble and needed to pretend she had the authority in a situation. Over the years Samantha discovered it was simply Addie's way of flailing like a wounded animal backed into a corner. When the diaper line came out, Samantha knew she was actually the one with the upper hand, whether or not Addie realized it.

Fighting back a smile, Samantha said, "All right. Then what *would* you like me to say?"

"I want you to find out who set my kitchen on fire. That's what I want."

She wouldn't let this go, would she? Samantha would have to make a whole charade of an investigation to appease Addie. Once again.

That should be simple enough. It just wasn't how she wanted to spend her time this week.

A spot of blue the shade Addie's apron caught Samantha's attention in the restaurant parking lot.

It was hair. Turquoise hair. Not exactly a regular

sight here in Etta, but someone's teenager could have easily ordered dye online, even if they couldn't find any in a store for fifty miles.

The owner of the hair closed the driver's side door of a gray compact car. They stood fairly still, looking at the building, assessing the damage. Some nosy onlooker, like the dozens she'd turned away earlier.

Samantha squinted. Not a teenager. A woman. Mid-to-late twenties. Short stature. Average build. She couldn't make out specifics from this distance, but she had a running mental record of every person living in this town. Blue hair or not, this person wasn't on Samantha's list. Most everyone who might have fit that description had fled this place years ago. Off to colleges or new jobs or bigger cities.

Oh, no.

"Did you hear a word I said?"

Samantha turned from the unwelcome sort-of-stranger to find Addie's hands in fists on both her hips.

No, no, no, no.

If Samantha was right about the owner of that hair, and if Addie caught even a whiff of her around here, this week would take a steep nosedive. If Addie already thought someone had messed with her restaurant...

"I'm sorry, Adeline. I was just running those statements through my head again to think if I missed anything."

"Oh. Well, then." That seemed to appease her. For now. "Did you come up with anything?"

Samantha shook her head. "No, ma'am, but I promise you I will take this all into careful consideration. If this was anything but an accident, I'll get to the bottom of it."

Good thing it really was just an accident.

But if Addie caught sight of that hair and the person attached to it, Samantha might end up with an assault case on her hands. Or worse. This town held grudges like nothing else. And they sure as hell didn't like anything or anyone who didn't "fit." From everything Samantha remembered, Erin Sonnier most definitely did not "fit" here.

But she and her grandfather had been quite the pair, and that gentle soul would have taken down anyone who disparaged her. Like everyone else, Samantha had expected Erin to handle everything she could from a distance. Surely the woman wouldn't have stepped foot back in this town if she didn't have to.

Samantha put a hand on Addie's arm and gently walked her behind the restaurant where the volunteer firefighters were clearing out. "I'm going to go out front to check on a few more things, then I've got to head back to the station to file these statements. I'll be in touch if I have any more questions. Did you call your insurance yet?"

Addie's face dropped, and she began patting at her apron and pants. "Oh my Lord, no. Not yet. Now, where is my phone?"

Thank goodness. That should keep her occupied. At least long enough to keep her away from the front of the building and keep her from making *more* accusations while Samantha sent Erin on her way.

Samantha turned again but found the gray car alone. No blue hair. No Erin.

Crap.

Chapter Two

THE SMOKE SMELL was worse near the restaurant, but not as bad as Erin had expected. Most of the stench had been carried away. With the thick heat and lack of a breeze, Erin was surprised not to find smoke hovering over this area like a weighted blanket.

She peered inside the restaurant through the glass doors. The lights were on, but she didn't see anyone. A fire truck was parked along the road, and hoses lay on the ground beside the building, but it didn't look like there'd been much damage to the front of the restaurant.

Clearly, they weren't serving lunch. Didn't look like there were any staff vehicles left in the parking lot. So, she guessed she wasn't getting that sandwich.

Still, Erin wondered how much damage the place had actually taken. Maybe it was being back in this nosy-ass place, but she really wanted to see what happened now that she was here.

"That would be a mistake."

Erin froze with her palm on the door handle and turned toward the woman's voice behind her.

The woman maintained a casual stance with a clipboard held against her thigh. Her hair was pulled back in a low, straight ponytail, and she wore a light khaki, short-sleeved button-down shirt with surprisingly well-fitted, dark khaki pants.

Great, a cop.

Erin and this town and cops didn't have a great history.

The woman's dark eyes narrowed on Erin. She clearly wasn't in the mood for any more bullshit than she'd already seen today.

Those eyes.

Erin knew those eyes. Or at least she'd seen them before. She checked out the name patch on the woman's uniform. Sergeant Ardoin. The last name was familiar, since it was so common around here, but her memory couldn't attach it to any women who would match this age and description.

Erin pulled it together and asked innocently, "Are they closed?"

"The fire truck and empty parking lot weren't enough clues for you?"

A tiny zing ran through Erin.

Sass. She liked this woman already.

Too bad she couldn't remember her.

Oh, crap. *Should* she remember her?

Was she mistaking sass for contempt? Resentment? Unresolved grudges?

"Have a mad craving for a BLT."

The woman's face softened. "Well, you won't get one here today. And I really wouldn't go in there if I were you."

Erin eyed her curiously. "Did someone get hurt?"

Now she felt bad. Shit, she hated feeling bad for anyone in this town.

"No," the woman said. "It's just that Addie's on a tear. Looking for someone to pin the accident on."

Erin instinctively surveyed the area to see if anyone else was around looking for a scapegoat. She should have known better than to make an appearance anywhere besides her grandfather's place.

The woman took a step closer and peered inside the building. "I reminded her to call her insurance, but she'll be wrapping that up soon. Better if she doesn't spot you here."

Better for Erin, for sure. She'd wanted to slip into town unnoticed, take care of her business, and slip back out as soon as possible. Addie stirring up gossip and dropping accusations at her door would slow everything down.

But why did this woman care one way or another? Why was she on a covert mission to warn Erin about Addie?

"Sorry, I've been gone a while," she said. "Do I know you?"

The woman held out her hand. Arm straight. Right hand in a tight line perpendicular to the ground. Erin was sure she could slice through metal with that hand.

"Samantha. We went to high school together. I was Samantha Keller back then."

Erin caught something in the woman's face that she couldn't quite identify. Some kind of discomfort. Erin hated when she couldn't read someone. She didn't exactly *like* people, but reading people was a useful skill she'd honed over the years. Easier to get exactly what you want if you know what the other person is thinking or feeling.

She shook the woman's hand and was surprised by the soft but confident grip she received in return. She'd expected the woman to strangle her hand with that initial stance, but she'd wrapped her soft, warm hand around Erin's and gave the gentlest of squeezes.

Wait...

That maiden name finally registered in Erin's brain.

"Sam?"

The woman nodded.

Well, this day was just getting better and better. Of all the annoying things she could have guessed would cross her path here, she never would have guessed she'd be cornered outside a restaurant fire by a former Keller turned police officer.

The Kellers were one of the oldest and richest families in Etta. Well, rich by Etta standards. But it wasn't the money that mattered around here as much as the power. And the Kellers had all of it. Money *and* power.

"I swear this was not me." Just being in this place made her defensive, and being in the presence of a Keller family cop made her downright jumpy. Even a Keller she didn't fully remember yet.

She wished her brain would catch up quicker, but its fancy trick of blocking access to her past was a well-trained self-defense mechanism. One she was normally grateful for.

Samantha laughed. "I know. It was a total accident. Grease fire." She aimed a thumb at the restaurant. "But you know that won't stop her from throwing the blame your way."

"Right." Erin assessed the woman in front of her. She vaguely remembered Samantha Keller. Sam, everyone called her. She was two years ahead of Erin and ran with a completely different crowd. More like Samantha ran with an actual crowd and Erin ran with herself, mostly. "I'm not trying to be rude, but I don't get why you care whether or not Addie serves me up for lunch."

Samantha smiled. A beautiful, wide smile that brightened her rich, tanned complexion. "Would you believe I'm not a big fan of unnecessary paperwork?"

It was Erin's turn to smile. That she could relate to.

Although her fuzzy memories of Samantha didn't line up with that statement. She remembered her as the type to fall in line and care about grades and all of that.

"You remember me?" Erin was used to people remembering the rumors about her, but not actually her. "I didn't think we had any classes together."

"Just an art class. And you went out with one of my friends right before you left town. Julie Myers."

Oof. That she remembered.

Specifically, she remembered it not ending well. None of her relationships here had ended well, so at least she'd left a consistent reputation behind.

"I wasn't sure it was you at first." That smile again. "But when you said why you were here... well, your BLT cravings are pretty notorious."

Erin suddenly remembered that she'd broken up with Julie Myers over a BLT. Julie had tried not to cry, but tears spilled out anyway while Erin finished her sandwich. Addie really did make a killer BLT.

She could remember that breakup sandwich, but she couldn't remember much about Samantha Keller. She'd spent most of her own high school days experimenting with whatever she could get her hands on. Anything that got her high and made it easier to forget she lived in this place. She kept to herself and ignored most of her classmates, so it wasn't a surprise that she didn't remember much about Samantha besides her name.

But that smile and that handshake and those sweet, soulful eyes kind of made Erin wish she could remember more.

Probably better this way, though. Nothing good could come from crushing on a cop. Especially a cop from *this* town with *that* last name. Even if Samantha clearly didn't use it anymore.

Plus, the new name indicated that this woman was probably married.

A married cop was definitely off the menu.

"Well, I'd better high-tail it out of here before Addie shows up."

Sam's smile faded. "I'm sorry about your grandfather. I remember you two were close."

Close. Yeah, they'd been close. Closest she'd been to anyone since her parents died all those years ago.

"Thanks." She cleared her throat and pointed at her car. "I'd better get to the house. Lots to do."

"Right. Well, it was good seeing you again."

"Yeah, you too," Erin said. "Thanks for the warning. About Addie and all."

"No problem. You take care."

Erin managed to pull herself away from that smile and walked back to her car, where she turned on the ignition and cranked up the air conditioner. While she waited for the car to cool off from its brief stay in the unbearable August heat, Erin took a big swig of Dr. Pepper.

Her stomach growled. At least it had the courtesy to wait until she was in the car.

She watched as Samantha walked in the opposite direction toward the back of the restaurant. The woman made even gross khaki cop pants look good. Like... real good.

Too bad she was a cop.

And a Keller.

A married Keller at that.

While Erin was admiring the woman's ass, Adeline Weaver walked out from the back of her restaurant. She

17

met up with Samantha and began rattling on about something, her hands flailing in the air as she spoke.

That was enough of a cue for Erin.

She capped her drink, put the car in reverse, then peeled out of the parking lot before that old bat could get a good look at her.

Chapter Three

SAMANTHA COLLAPSED in her chair and stared at the stacks of paper on her desk, while Connie's dark fingers—decked out this week in purple polish with sparkly gold jewels—clicked away on the keyboard across the room. Connie was the station's administrative assistant and the most vital cog in their whole operation. She'd been a fixture in this office for as long as Samantha could remember, long before Samantha ever worked there herself.

Connie raised an eyebrow at Samantha, her way of asking how much extra work this most recent call would pile on her plate. She cleared her throat and asked in her deep, raspy voice, "Everything okay at Addie's?"

"Everything but one section of her kitchen," Samantha said with a nod. "Looks like just a fryer accident. Fire team put it out before too much damage, at least."

Samantha said another tiny, silent prayer of thanks

that she'd convinced Addie *not* to file that ridiculous accusation against her staff. The last thing she needed this week was a paperwork trail of the woman's conspiracy theories. Theories Samantha would have to at least appear to follow up on if they'd been in ink or in the database. Now that she'd appealed to Addie's decency, she could file this, leave the case open for a few days to make a show of it, and mark it closed before the end of next week since no actual crime had been committed.

The door chimed as it opened and her two coworkers breezed into the station, chuckling over something or other.

"Hey, Sam." Dustin greeted her with his charming twenty-four-year-old grin, complete with that adorable dimple. Samantha liked him enough, in a little brother/puppy kind of way. He was cheerful, diligent, and eager to please. Good thing, since he was the only other full-time officer at the station. "How was your fire call? We could see the smoke from across town."

"Wasn't too bad. I had more trouble putting out Addie than the firemen had putting out that grease fire, though."

Dustin cringed. "That doesn't sound fun."

"You two sound like you had fun, though." She'd tried to leave the annoyance out of her voice but suspected it was apparent, anyway.

She normally hated PR appearances, and most days she'd gladly choose calming a conspiracy-fueled Addie over shaking hands. But it would have been helpful to get her face in the paper this week. Especially if it meant getting her sister off her back.

Samantha was already weary of all the campaign appearances her sister insisted she couldn't say no to, and the endless string of them never seemed to be enough for her sister-turned-campaign manager. Small-town politics wasn't a huge beast like in bigger cities, but it was still a game here. A game Samantha's sister continuously reminded her she needed to play if she wanted to win.

And she did want to win the election.

Just not for the prestige or power that came with the title.

"Eh, it was okay. Same old, same old," her boss, Police Chief Gary Vidrine, said as he tapped her desk on the way to his office. He was shorter than Dustin, made more apparent by the shoulder hunch of a man weeks from retirement. "You'll see soon enough."

"If the-same-old means cake at every one of these things, maybe I want to be Chief. Is it too late to enter the race?" Dustin winked at Samantha, so she wadded up a sticky note and threw it at him.

Chief Vidrine chuckled. "Think you can manage to get back to work after all that cake excitement?"

"Yes, sir," said Dustin, finding his way to his own desk.

Connie handed Chief Vidrine a printout as he passed. As usual, she was completely uninterested in their conversation or any gossip that entered the office and carried on with her own work.

Chief Vidrine retreated to his office to catch up on missed calls and notes.

Samantha didn't envy that part of his job, either. She didn't want the phone calls, cameras, or the cake that came with being Etta's Chief of Police. Samantha just wanted to help people.

Sure, she helped people nearly every day already, but as Chief she could make a bigger impact on the town. She could be part of the decisions that made life better for *all* of Etta's citizens. Especially for the citizens who were so often overlooked or flat-out ignored.

But first, she had to win this election. And that meant beating her old nemesis: Jordan Fonseca.

Samantha frowned at the half-filed paperwork on her desk. She couldn't beat him or win this election if she couldn't close a simple case or manage an over-the-top restaurant owner.

An image of Erin flashed in her mind. The blue hair that matched Adeline's apron and mimicked those bright blue eyes dancing with mischief.

Yup, that was the Erin she remembered from high school.

Erin had been a couple years behind her, but it had been a slight stretch of the truth when she'd said she knew her from dating her friend. That had been true, of course, but Erin had been on her radar long before that. And after.

Everyone knew who Erin was after The Incident, but Samantha remembered her from art class junior year. Samantha had needed the requirement to graduate, but it was clearly Erin's passion, even though she'd been a freshman. Samantha remembered how intensely those blue eyes would focus on a canvas. How Erin would get little flecks of paint in her then-blonde hair. How she never even realized there were ten other people in the room with her.

Outside of the studio, Erin attracted attention even when she wasn't trying to. She was a tractor beam for trouble.

The last thing either of them needed this week was trouble.

Erin had enough on her plate dealing with her grandfather's death and clearing out that house without Adeline and the rest of town stirring up mess. And Samantha sure as heck didn't need to clean up that mess.

It would be a lot easier if she could handle anything that landed Erin's way quickly and quietly... before the whole town lit up like wildfire.

"I missed a signature on one of these statements," she said, grabbing a random paper and holding it up for show. "I'm going to head out a few minutes early and take care of it on my way home."

"A missed signature?" Dustin raised his eyebrows and let out a low whistle. "Slipping there, Sergeant?"

She pointed at him on her way out. "Got some icing on your face."

He wiped at his face as she waved goodbye to Connie and headed out the door.

~

Erin stood in front of the porch steps and stared at the big blue Acadian-style home. It looked the same on the outside, despite not seeing it in over five years.

Her grandfather had always kept up with the place until he couldn't do everything himself anymore. By then, he'd built up enough good karma to have a line of volunteers willing to run a tractor over the field or fix a loose porch deck board or drag a dead possum out from under the house.

A tiny ping of guilt pricked at Erin's gut for not being around to do some of those things, but she squashed that emotion like she always did. Grandpa Sonnier had insisted that it wasn't her job to take care of him. It was *his* job to take care of *her* until she could fully take care of herself, and then she was her own responsibility.

Erin wondered when that day would come. Because she sure as hell wasn't doing her end of the bargain. Not yet, at least.

And now she had to take care of... this.

Everything.

His house. His possessions. His bank accounts. His investments... did he even have investments?

Erin climbed the steps and stood on the solid porch. The place really was in good shape, considering its age.

A grotesque squawk rang out through the closed door and through the thick August evening air.

That bird.

She'd have an easier time finding a buyer for this house than finding someone to take that feathered hell-beast.

She fumbled for the right key and opened the lock. The knob was new, but it had been keyed to match the old lock. He could have just as easily given her a new key, but knowing him, he'd wanted to make sure she could get in any time she wanted or needed.

Bet he hadn't planned for this, though.

Once inside, the memories hit her as hard as the scent of birdseed and feathers. She'd left town almost ten years ago. Five years since she'd been back at all. But she'd grown up here, lived in this place as long as she could remember. Not that she remembered much at all before the accident.

There was a before. And then there was an after. Here. Almost all of her memories were of Grandpa Sonnier and this house.

The bird squawked again. This time with a hearty, "McFlyyyyyy."

Her trip down memory lane would have to wait, apparently. Just as well. She didn't want to deal with anything else yet. It hadn't been a long drive, but she was exhausted just stepping foot in this town.

Her stomach growled. Dang fire ruining her dinner options.

She headed toward the living room and found Marty McFly bobbing his head and pacing on his perch in excitement.

"Good to see you too, buddy."

She stuck her finger near the cage, and Marty hobbled over and placed his beak around it, his tongue tasting her. He released and squawked, "McFlyyyyyy!!!"

Grandpa had always wanted a bird, and he'd been researching them for years before he found just the breed he wanted: a blue Quaker parrot. Once Erin had gotten her license and wasn't around the house much anymore, he found one at a pet store in the city. To keep him company, he'd said. She always swore he got that thing just to piss her off, but she knew he loved it. More than her, she'd accused more than once. It was embarrassing to recall now because everyone knew that was a lie.

"He remembers you."

Erin spun around and gripped her keys in her fist, thankful she hadn't tucked them away or placed her only potential weapon on a table out of reach. But she quickly relaxed when she saw her intruder.

"Zach." She released a heavy sigh of relief. "You scared the crap out of me."

He shrugged. The tiny watering can in his right hand caught her eye as it rose and fell with the motion. "I told you I'd be here."

"Yeah, in general. But I didn't think you were *in the house*. Like right at this moment."

Zachary Hebert lived a quarter mile down her grandfather's little country road. His family had lived there all his life, long before Erin had moved in here.

His family had always been close with Grandpa, checking in on him, stopping by for coffee, or whatever people did out here. But his parents were both gone now. His mom had died of cancer when they were in high school, and his dad had remarried and moved to Texas a few years ago. Zach kept the house and apparently kept up the tradition of checking in on Grandpa.

Zach had found her number in Grandpa's phone and was the first to contact her. Making that the second worst day of her life.

"Sorry." He ran a hand through his dark, wavy hair. "Didn't mean to startle you. Didn't know you'd be in today. Been coming every evening after work to check on Marty and water the plants."

"Right. Thanks."

She wanted to tell him he could have let the house plants die for all she cared. But doing this seemed important to him. His expression told her he took this responsibility very seriously.

He looked almost exactly as she'd remembered. Slightly taller than her, but so was everyone else. Muscular, but soft. Farm muscles. And dark eyes most people couldn't read. But Erin always could.

He was a couple of years younger than her, but when she'd first moved in with Grandpa, Zach had been her only friend. The only person in town who'd talk to her. Everyone else was afraid she was cursed or something. Like they could catch her dead parents or her tragic tale.

Other than that, she and Zach never had much in common, and the friendship didn't last into high school. Erin had only cared about art and, later, making out and getting high. Zach had cared about chores and homework and serious stuff. He'd been a nice kid, and she'd liked him more than she'd liked most people around here. They'd just grown apart over the years.

She was glad to see he looked good. Healthy? Happy maybe?

He glanced around the room. "I should go. Let you get settled."

Settled? She didn't plan on staying one second longer than she had to, so there was no need to get settled.

But she sure as hell didn't want to make small talk about the only thing they had in common at this point. Her dead Grandpa. Their dead parents. Death, death, death. They could form a little death squad. *That* sounded fun.

The bird let out a high-pitched tone, mimicking something obnoxious in this house that she would soon discover.

"Is there anywhere else to get food around here? I'm sure there's nothing edible left in that fridge, and it seems I've lost my go-to sandwich fix."

"You heard about Addie's then."

"Yeah, I stopped for gas and saw smoke, so I walked over. Not too bad, but looks like it'll be closed for a while."

"You did *not* walk your butt over to the scene of a fire."

Erin cringed. "I kind of did. But Sam warned me Addie was on a tear."

"Ah, so you've met Captain Tight Pants." He fought back a way-too-proud-of-himself grin.

"Sergeant Tight Pants, I believe." She grinned with him. "And yes. Yes, I did."

28

Zach gave her a sly, sideways smile. "I remember that look."

"What look?"

She didn't have a look. Did she?

"You, Erin Sonnier, are *smitten*."

"Am not." Erin rolled her eyes. "Cops are never on the menu. Weren't you leaving?"

He laughed. "As for the menu, Addie's was pretty much it at this time unless you want to drive half an hour out of town. I can bring you some stuff from my place. Hold you over 'til you get to the store?"

"Thanks, but I'll be fine. Got a granola bar in my bag. I've got to go into town tomorrow anyway, so I'll figure it out then."

"All right." He nodded and headed toward the door. "You know where to find me if you change your mind or need anything else. And you've got my number."

"Sure do. Thanks."

He paused in the doorway. "Good to see you, Erin."

"You too, Zach."

And it was. To her utter surprise, it really did feel good to see him. He'd scared the piss out of her, but he'd made her initial return to this house feel a lot less cold and lonely than it could have been.

Now though, once the door shut behind him, Zach was gone, leaving Erin alone with this too-big house and her too-heavy memories.

"McFlyyyyy!"

And that blasted bird.

Erin sighed and looked around the place. The sun

was just beginning to lower in the sky, sending an intense beam of light through the sheer living room curtains. She retreated into the much darker kitchen and opened the refrigerator.

As she'd guessed, the fridge was empty. Like... way emptier than she'd suspected. Zach must have cleared out anything perishable.

She made a mental note to do something nice for him.

But what? She couldn't very well hand him some dangly earrings, which were her go-to thoughtful, hand-made gift. What did nice people do for one another as a thank you? Not like he could use a Starbucks gift card around here. Fruit basket? Cake? If Addie's reopened soon, maybe she could buy him lunch.

A knock on the front door jarred her out of her gift-pondering. Zach probably forgot something.

She peered around the curtain, and her chest fluttered. A sensation she'd been unacquainted with for a very long time.

Erin stiffened her shoulders and grabbed the door-knob, pausing briefly to give herself a pep talk.

Keep it together. You're here to sell a house, not flirt with a married woman.

With her priorities in check, Erin opened the door for Sergeant Tight Pants.

Chapter Four

"HI."

Samantha waved awkwardly. She'd completely lost her ability to speak more than that.

What had she even come here for?

All she could focus on were those crystal blue eyes that... was she imagining this... appeared glad to see her.

That couldn't be right. No one was ever glad to see the police show up unannounced. No one, but especially not Erin Sonnier. And Samantha hadn't even run home to change, so she was still wearing her uniform. She'd had the time, but she hadn't *wanted* to take the time to change. All she'd wanted to do was get here.

For the case.

Right.

"Is something wrong?" Erin asked.

Wrong? Yes, something was very wrong. This overwhelming urge to kiss Erin Sonnier was very, very wrong.

Samantha was running for Chief of Police, and the

Chief of Police couldn't run around kissing citizens during unannounced house calls.

But Erin wasn't technically a citizen of Etta...

Samantha held up the paper bag in her hand. "I just wanted to bring you this."

Erin took the bag hesitantly. Her eyes lit up as she peered inside, and a smile played at the corners of her tiny mouth. But suspicion lingered in her voice. "You brought me a sandwich?"

"Consider it your Welcome Back to Etta basket." Samantha lifted onto her toes, then rocked back on her heels. "I felt bad that you couldn't get one earlier, and I know that with all you have to do, things can't be easy. Plus, I figured you probably didn't have anything in the fridge here."

Erin poked inside the bag. "It's... a BLT." Her voice cracked the tiniest bit at the edges of those letters. "Thanks. Where did you find one? Zach said nothing was open around here."

"Tiny lunch place by the station. The owner was still inside, and he owed me a favor. *Still* owes me a favor, but we agreed on this as a favor down payment." She tried not to sound too pleased with herself.

"I appreciate it." Erin nodded inside. "Do you want to come in? You were right about not much being here, but I think I saw a few root beers in the fridge."

YES.

"I probably shouldn't."

"Sure you should." Erin opened the door wider. "Come in for a minute. I insist."

Against her better judgment, Samantha stepped inside. Her brain was running in twenty different directions, reminding her of all the reasons she shouldn't be in here and all the reasons she really wanted to be in that house with Erin right now.

But her mind quieted once she was fully inside. It was like stepping through the wardrobe into Narnia.

Michael Sonnier had collected all kinds of vintage memorabilia. And not just cheesy Burger King glassware or plastic Coca-Cola polar bears. Everything in this home was the real deal, purchased at rural estate sales and, later, on eBay.

This was why she'd agreed to linger for a minute. Her curiosity couldn't resist the pull of this place. She'd been inside only once before, to take his statement after he'd witnessed an accident on the road in front of his house, and everything was exactly as she remembered.

Sure. This was why she'd taken Erin's invitation to come inside.

"Yeah, it's a lot," Erin said.

"It's great. Very him." Everything was meticulously placed and in mint condition. She wouldn't be surprised if he also kept a detailed ledger of every single item in his collection. She spotted the cage hanging from the ceiling near the edge of the living room. "I see Marty's still here."

"You should have heard him when I got here. The damn thing must have worn himself out."

Samantha followed Erin into the kitchen, but declined when offered a can of root beer.

"You sure?"

Samantha nodded. "I really should head back out soon. I just—"

Her phone chimed in its holder at her waist. When she pulled it out and looked at the screen, she regretted not putting the phone on silent and ignoring it. Even though it wasn't exactly a thing she could do with her job.

"Problem?" Erin asked.

Dinner Sunday. Here. 6pm.

It was more of a summons than an invitation. But coming from her mother, that was fitting.

"Just a family thing."

"Sooooo definitely a problem."

Samantha looked up from her phone to see that playful smile she remembered Teen Erin walking around with so often. It was a rock candy smile. All pretty and sweet, but sharp and could secretly cut the roof of your mouth.

Erin knew exactly how to flash that smile to get what she wanted. Samantha knew this. Even so, here she was.

Thankfully, Samantha's phone chimed again before she could ponder what Erin might want from her.

WARNING: Mom's doing a dinner thing! She's summoning us all to the compound this weekend. Bring your gun. And the handcuffs. FUN TIMES AHEAD.

This one Samantha laughed at. "My sister this time." She put her phone on silent and tucked it away. She'd deal with them both and turn the volume back on later.

Erin bit her lip and narrowed her eyes, deep in thought. "Melissa?"

"Melanie."

"Right." That smile returned. "The only other acceptable Keller, if I remember correctly." She paused, but the smile never left. "No offense."

"You're not wrong. Assuming the other bit meant me."

Erin laughed softly. "Of course."

Oh, for crap's sake, Sam, get a hold of yourself.

But all she really wanted to get a hold of right now was the woman in front of her.

Completely unacceptable.

"Then I agree whole-heartedly with your assessment of my family." Samantha lowered her head and her voice. "Just don't tell any of them I said that."

"If you carry a gun and are still afraid of them, what hope is there for the rest of us?"

"That I have everyone else's backs?"

Erin's eyes narrowed, disbelief clear in her expression as she chewed on Sam's statement.

Eventually, an amused smile reappeared. "You really believe that, don't you?"

Samantha blinked at her a few times, then said, "Of course I do."

It was the one thing she truly did believe. Because if she didn't believe it, who else would make things better around here? Who else would fight for the people of Etta?

Sure, it was a tall order for one person, but what else was she supposed to do?

Awkward silence filled the space between them. Samantha was fully aware of it worming its way between them, filling more and more time and growing by the second, but her awareness didn't help her one bit in trying to fill it.

Then she remembered the *real* reason she'd come here. Or at least her excuse.

"I actually came by to give you this." She pulled a card from her pocket and handed it to Erin. "My card. And number. If you need it."

Erin's smile fell and her eyes widened in confusion as she slowly reached for the card. Or maybe it was fear? Samantha couldn't tell, but it was a very not good look in those eyes of hers.

"Um... thanks."

"If you have any trouble." Samantha stumbled over her words like an awkward teenager.

"Trouble?"

"If Addie stirs up anything or the rumor mill takes over and anyone hassles you about the fire. Just let me know, and I'll take care of it."

"You want me to tattle on the meanies?"

When she put it that way, it did sound pretty ridiculous. "Sometimes the meanies need it pointed out that they're being meanies."

Erin's expression relaxed a little, and she waved the card in the air. "Thanks. This feels like a lot of power to have."

Samantha laughed. When was the last time she'd laughed this much? With anyone? Much less over something as small as a business card?

"Use it wisely," she teased. Somehow, she managed to hold back the accompanying wink she was inclined to deliver with that line. "Well, I'd better head out."

"Are you sure you have to?"

Was that disappointment in her voice? And in her eyes?

"Yeah. I'm sure you have a lot to do here, so I'm gonna get out of your way."

"If you stay, I can pretend I don't have to do anything a little longer."

"I can't be responsible for that." She nodded at her card Erin had placed on a counter. "Let me know if you need anything while you're here."

"Will do," Erin said. "Thanks for the sandwich."

Samantha took a step backward toward the door. She pressed her lips together and gave a tight nod before she had a chance to say anything else.

Anything inappropriate.

Anything she shouldn't say while she was in uniform.

Anything close to what she was actually thinking and feeling about Erin Sonnier right now.

Chapter Five

ERIN STOOD in line behind three octogenarians. This was probably what counted as "busy" for the town clerk's office.

She was honestly surprised she had to wait at all on a Thursday afternoon. She would have been here first thing if she'd realized she needed so many extra copies of Grandpa's death certificate. Erin had no idea why they couldn't make a copy of the one she had or why they couldn't just look at it and say, "Yep, all good." Then everyone could move on with their lives.

Particularly, so she could get back to her real life in New Orleans.

Except New Orleans didn't have a certain gorgeous sergeant who apparently made sandwich deliveries.

She really needed to get that woman out of her head. Nothing good could come from crushing on Samantha.

The old man in front of her shuffled forward several steps as an old lady with a cane finished at the window and hobbled out of the building. She gave a drunk-looking grin at Erin as she walked past. Probably a friend of Grandpa's who recognized her.

A reminder that this place was too damn small. She missed the anonymity of New Orleans. Most people out there treated her like family, but they didn't actually know her history.

Ten minutes later, with her feet aching from standing in one place, it was finally her turn at the counter.

"Next."

To her surprise, the voice didn't belong to a middle-aged white woman with a scowl and grudge from spending half her life at that window.

Erin didn't recognize the young black man across the counter. He was probably a couple years younger than her, and since she didn't recognize him from school, she assumed he moved here some time after she left town.

There was a hint of curiosity in his gaze, like he was looking at some weird exhibit. Extra weird since Etta didn't have a single museum of any kind. Not exactly a beacon of culture.

"Nice hair." His voice was deep, but sweet. It had a lightness that was super rare in this town. Everyone here was rundown, bored, or jaded.

Since she didn't detect any sarcasm in his tone, she simply said, "Thanks."

"What can I help you with?"

"I need copies of a death certificate."

"Direct relative?"

"Next of kin," she replied.

He nodded and reached into the cubbies beside him. He pulled out a sheet of paper and handed it to her. "Here's the request application. Do you know how many copies you'll need? They're nine dollars each, and we usually recommend getting extra. People always forget some place and end up needing more copies than they think."

How many places had the attorney told her she'd need them for when she called earlier that morning? She was the sole beneficiary, so he'd promised things should be fairly simple. But she still needed to file a whole bunch of paperwork at a whole bunch of places. The bank, life insurance, V.A., social security, taxes... and something else maybe that she couldn't remember.

"Five should be good. I'll just get more later if I need them."

"You might want to order extra now. You don't want to have to go through all of this again."

"All of what?" She processed the first part of his explanation, then said, "Order? What do you mean order extra? Can't you print some back there while I wait?"

He chuckled, his eyes filled with amusement rather than the judgment she was used to around here. "The request takes ten to twelve days. Someone has to go over your request, make sure you're actually entitled to copies, then the copies have to be certified before we can release them to you."

"Certified," she repeated. "Doesn't that just mean someone presses one of those seal thingies on a corner?"

He smiled, laughter still playing at the edge of his

mouth. She didn't like being laughed at, but it seemed more like he found this whole process as ridiculous as she did and was happy to have someone in on the joke who wasn't berating him or demanding to speak to a manager. "Pretty much."

Ten to twelve days would put a major wrench in her plans to get out of here fast. But she could work on getting the house ready to sell while she waited to close all of Grandpa's accounts. "Can you mail them to me? In New Orleans?"

"Just write the address you want them sent to on the form. It's an extra fifty cents if you want to mail them rather than pick them up, although you'll get them faster if you pick up the copies when they're ready."

"Well, hopefully I won't be anywhere near here in ten days."

He smiled and nodded. "Understood."

Erin unlocked the front door to the short, piercing screech of "McFly!"

"Hey, Marty. Missed me?"

"McFlyyyyyyyyyy."

She'd take that as a yes. Damn bird. The last thing she needed was a headache from his screeching.

She tossed her keys and phone on an end table and crossed the living room to Marty's cage. He danced and paced and squawked while she slid up the little door for the birdseed.

Jeez, chill dude.

She didn't want to deal with this thing—exactly why she didn't want a pet of her own—but the sooner she took care of Marty, the sooner she could get off her feet and plan her next steps to get out of this town.

Erin made sure the seed door was shut before heading to the kitchen. Even more than a headache, the absolute last thing she needed was a rogue parrot flying around the house, shitting everywhere and refusing to go back in his cage. She'd probably get the dang bird killed. And while she didn't exactly want him around, she also couldn't handle the guilt of Grandpa's dead parrot on her hands.

Erin shook that thought away and dumped the seed shells in the kitchen trash can.

Shit.

She'd forgotten to ask Zach where Grandpa kept the supplies for Marty. She crossed her fingers and headed to the linen closet in the hall.

Bingo.

She should have known they'd be in the same place. Grandpa always put so much thought into how he organized things that once something was placed, that's where it stayed, because he'd selected the perfect location to begin with.

For some reason, the linen closet was the perfect location for bird seed and papers and everything else Marty-related. It made sense for a man with only two beds and only one back-up pair of sheets for each. He only needed one shelf for those and space for two extra pillows. The rest of the tiny closet was all Marty's domain.

Erin refilled the cup using a tiny scoop she found with the seed. The gigantic plastic container was filled with way more food than she would need until she found a new home for the guy. She hoped. Someone in this town had to want Marty, right? For sentimental reasons, if nothing else.

She returned the seed cup to Marty's cage then took the poop paper from the tray and replaced it with a fresh one. Finally, she changed out the water and checked that all exit points were secured.

"There you go, buddy."

Marty bobbed his headed and continued pacing and freaking out, screaming his name at the top of his lungs.

Sheesh. Erin had no idea how Grandpa put up with this thing, much less loved the creature.

Her phone rang from the end table. Erin picked it up when she saw Zach's name on the screen.

"Hello," she shouted over the squawking.

He chuckled. "Sounds like you and Marty are getting along swell."

"Super," she said. "What on earth is his deal? Was he always like this and I just forgot?"

"Kind of," said Zach. "On and off. I mean, he's a bird. They're all obnoxious, in my opinion."

"Believe me, in my opinion, too."

"But he's been a little more unsettled. Since... you know."

Erin glanced over at the bird. Poor Marty. She should

have realized he'd miss Grandpa. Of course he would.

"I was calling to check on you and see how things were going."

"Just grand," she said, her voice dripping with the sarcasm that had been festering all day.

"Did you just get back?"

"Yeah, walked in a few minutes ago."

"That could be why he's so excited."

Erin looked down and saw a smudge of white gloopy bird poop on her hand. "Great. This day keeps getting better."

"So I guess I shouldn't ask how today went."

"Today went fine," she said on her way to the bathroom. "I crossed some things off the list, so I guess that counts as fine."

Never mind that crossing things off just added more things to the to-do list. Not to mention those extra ten to twelve days. At this rate, she would never settle Grandpa's estate and escape this place.

She flipped on the light and switched the phone to speaker. Then she placed it on the counter and ran the water, double-checking that she'd turned the cold water on because it came out warm, nearly hot. Exposed pipes and August heat. Fun combination.

"Did you just take me to the *bathroom* with you? I didn't know we were that close."

"We aren't. Calm down." She finished her scrub and shut off the water. "I'm washing my—"

She froze mid-water-shake-off when she spotted something in the mirror behind her. Something that should most definitely not be in her grandfather's bathroom with her.

"Holy crap!"

She stumbled toward the door, one hand on the knob behind her, the other hand up defensively in front of her. But it didn't look like she needed it.

"Erin? Erin?" Zach's voice echoed through the bathroom from the phone speaker. "Are you okay?"

She wasn't sure how to say *there's a giant man slumped beside the toilet in here with me* without tipping off said man that she'd noticed him. But from the look of him, it might not matter what she said or did at this point.

"I'm okay," she said. "I think."

"You think? Erin, what's going on? Talk to me."

"There's... a man. In the bathroom."

"*WHAT?!*"

She ignored Zach's shriek of concern and took a step toward the man and the toilet. He was slumped downward, wedged between the toilet and the wall. His pants were on—thank heavens for small favors—so it didn't look like a heart attack mid-dump.

Why would a man be taking a dump in Grandpa's bathroom in the first place???

She reached a leg toward the guy and nudged his backside with her foot.

No response. No flinch. No nothing.

Her heart beat fiercely in her chest, and her breath came in fast, shallow pants.

"Zach? I'm gonna have to call you back."

Chapter Six

SAMANTHA NODDED CURTLY and stepped inside as a pale, shaken Erin opened her door wide and gestured down the hall. Under better circumstances, it might have been a thrill to see her two days in a row. But she took no joy in seeing Erin like this.

Or in whatever Samantha was about to find in that bathroom.

When she called, Erin only said she'd found a man in her grandfather's bathroom. Dead, she thought. Erin said he hadn't moved, and she didn't see any signs that he was breathing. Samantha had wanted to stay on the cell with Erin, but she needed to request backup and an ambulance, just in case whoever this was still had a chance. Since Samantha had been nearby checking on Addie and the restaurant, she'd beaten everyone else to the scene.

"Stay here, please," she said, leaving Erin in the living room.

The bathroom light was on. Samantha slowed her approach and reached for her gun. When she peered around the corner, it was clear she didn't need it. The man was still slumped face down and wedged between the toilet and the wall, just as Erin had described in that eerily calm voice during their call a few minutes ago.

She kept her gun out but aimed it upward as she reached with her other hand to find a pulse. It was difficult, but she managed to lean awkwardly over his body and reach his neck.

Definitely dead, although how she couldn't tell yet. She had a good idea who this guy was, even if it made absolutely no sense.

She returned her gun to its holster and pulled out her radio. "Cancel that ambulance. We're gonna need the coroner instead."

When the confirmation came in, she used her phone to take photos of the body from several angles, as well as photos of the rest of the bathroom. Even without any signs of foul play, a dead intruder was suspicious enough.

Samantha tugged at the guy's shoulders to dislodge him. She was stronger than her lean, long frame led most people to assume, but this guy was a good two-hundred-fifty pounds of literal dead weight jammed into a corner.

Finally, she yanked him free and twisted him onto his back to lay the body on the floor in front of the toilet. She panted for a second, catching her breath while she studied the man.

"I know that guy!"

Samantha hung her head and sighed. "I thought I asked you to stay in the living room."

"Yeah, well, I don't work for you, and this is my house. Sort of."

Right. In addition to being the town's alleged petty arsonist, Erin was also known for being a not-great rule-follower. Especially not a polite-suggestion-follower. And now they could add not-great-request-follower to the list.

"That guy was in the gas station when I got into town. Would not shut up talking to that poor cashier," Erin said. "He *grunted* at me."

That sounded like Paul Latiolais. "You won't have to worry about his grunting anymore."

Samantha was surprised at how calm she was. Even by her own unflappable standards.

She didn't see a lot of death first-hand in this town. Most everyone died of old age or heart conditions or at the hospital after an accident. Very little of that fell under her jurisdiction.

But this was someone she knew, and he was somewhere he shouldn't be. Even if he'd died of natural causes, this was definitely her department.

No blood. No obvious bruising or other injuries. No signs of a struggle in the room.

Everything pointed to natural causes, but nothing about this scene looked natural.

A knock on Erin's door sent her out of the room, and Samantha took the opportunity to examine the body further. She felt around his head for lumps. Checked his torso under his shirt for signs of blood or wounds she might have missed. Then she examined his neck. No bruising there either.

Heart attack probably, if she had to guess at this point.

As Samantha released his head, her fingers grazed the skin along the sides of his neck, and she froze.

"It's just Zach from down the road!" Erin shouted from the front door.

Samantha leaned her head closer, studying where her finger had alerted her to something mildly suspicious.

There.

She squinted at the raised spot that could easily have been mistaken for a pimple or a bug bite. Except it had a tiny hole in the center and lacked the redness of a bug bite.

Crap.

Her brain went into overdrive, running through all the implications of that tiny spot on the man's neck.

She pulled out her radio once again and made the request she'd been hoping to avoid.

"Hey, Connie. Sam again. We're going to need the parish team out here."

"Excuse me," Erin said as she stood in the bathroom doorway, peering at Samantha talking into that blasted radio. "What does 'need the parish team' mean?"

Was this small-town lingo she'd forgotten or was it some kind of cop speak? Either way, Erin wanted to know what the ever-loving-heck was about to go down *in her house*.

Zach pushed against her back and peered over her shoulder. "Whoa. That *is* Paul. He's for real dead, huh?"

Samantha stood with her hands up as she walked toward them, pushing them out with an invisible wall. Her tight ponytail, the one that had looked super cute the day before, seemed extra tight and way less cute at the moment. Her dark eyes had carried a softness to them before, but now her vision was laser-focused. "We all need to go outside. Please."

"Fine." Erin shrugged Zach off and stepped backwards into the hallway. "But you didn't answer my question. What's this parish team business?"

She did *not* like being kept in the dark. On anything. Much less on the matter of a dead jerk in her house.

"No, I mean *outside the house*." Samantha practically growled as she herded them down the hallway. "And don't touch anything."

"Jeez. Fine." Erin turned around and gave Zach a shove toward the door when he tried to peek in the bathroom again. Then she froze. *Don't touch anything*. Realization dawned on her. "Shit, did someone kill him?"

The thought of one intruder dying in Grandpa's

house was enough of a shock. But *two* intruders? One a *murderer*???

"Wait, someone killed Paul?" Zach's voice rose in pitch with each word.

"I can't tell you anything for sure right now except we all need to step outside for a while."

"Who's the team from parish?" Erin asked. "Does that mean more cops in my house?"

Samantha pointed at the front door and followed them onto the porch just as an Etta cop car approached down the long gravel driveway, a cloud of limestone dust flanking it. "A team from the St. Dufour Parish Sheriff's Department is on their way. They have facilities and personnel to handle a case like this."

"Facilities?"

"For evidence. And analysis," Samantha said. "They might need to bring in the State Police, though. That'll be their call."

Samantha seemed calm. Jarringly calm, from Erin's point of view.

She'd half expected to witness some kind of pissing contest over the body. But Samantha didn't look ready for a fight. She just looked like a woman doing her job, as if this was the equivalent of filling out a spreadsheet.

Weren't cops supposed to be excited by big cases? Like, not happy someone died, but thrilled with the challenge. The kind of thing in a long list of things Erin did not find endearing about the profession and the people who flocked to it.

But Samantha looked more concerned than excited.

"You mean a whole mess of sheriffs and state police are coming here? Now?" Erin heard the shriek in her own voice. "And I have to stay outside while they drag this guy out of Grandpa's house?"

The house.

Who the hell would buy a house a guy *died* in? Possibly a murder house. In New Orleans, she'd have no problem. Might even be a selling point. But here? With these superstitious clowns around here?

Erin was screwed.

Not as screwed as Paul, but still. This didn't look good for her plan to get out of town quickly.

Zach put a hand on her arm. "It won't be that bad. Right, Sergeant Ardoin? They'll be out of here in a couple hours, I'm sure." He squeezed her arm gently, the reassuring touch warm and comforting, but not comforting enough under the circumstances. "And you can hang out at my place until they're done. I've got hot coffee and cold beer. Take your pick."

Erin was grateful for the offer. Really, she was. But hot coffee and cold beer wouldn't erase a murder.

"Listen, no offense to Paul back there because I know his day has been worse than mine, but I need this all over with. I'm in my dead Grandpa's house, where I just stumbled on a random dead guy, and it's all just too much." Erin's heart raced as the shock wore off. She took a deep breath and exhaled before she finished her rant, her words a little less confident and a little more shaky. "I just want them to hurry, so I can clean up behind them and get this place ready to sell. I've got the Realtor coming out tomorrow, and I want to make this whole nightmare go away."

She looked back at Samantha, the woman's dark eyes sympathetic and troubled now. Erin watched in horror as Samantha's lips moved to form the words, "Erin, I'm sorry. You can't put this house on the market yet. It's a crime scene."

Chapter Seven

THE FORENSICS CREW members were the first to arrive.

Samantha greeted them shortly after Zach convinced Erin to wait at his house. Poor Erin had been paler than Samantha had ever seen her. She couldn't remember Erin being afraid of anything, but finding Paul had clearly shaken her. Samantha had wanted to wrap her in a blanket and bring her tea.

But she had a case to run. A case that at first glance made absolutely no sense.

The only thing she could tell so far was it appeared that Paul had come in through the side door, through the kitchen. There were marks on the knob and frame that looked like forced entry.

Why Paul would want to break into this house, though, Samantha had no idea.

She led the team inside through the living room,

noting that other than a few soft squawks, that bird was eerily quiet. Must be traumatized along with Erin.

When Samantha showed the team the body, she explained exactly what she'd touched or moved and promised to forward her photos of the room from before all of that.

Then she went out to the porch to watch cars roll onto the property one after another with the sun hanging heavy and low on the horizon behind them.

Vultures.

She shouldn't be bitter or disparaging of fellow officers who were just doing their jobs. But handing the case over was the last thing she wanted to do, and she didn't plan on fully handing it over if she could help it.

"Sergeant Ardoin." The tall man's voice boomed across the yard as he slammed his cruiser door shut and headed toward her. His long strides made quick work of the distance and the porch steps, his toothy grin beaming in the mostly cloudless afternoon sun. "Got a bit of excitement all the way out in your little neck of the woods today, I see."

Little neck of the woods.

She shouldn't be surprised. This was how Jordan Fonseca was handling his entire campaign. Like he was some big shot, big city savior running for police chief of this sleepy little town. Not as the small parish deputy sheriff who was born and raised here and only pretended like he was some uppity big shot.

"Jordan." She nodded toward the house. "CSU beat you to it."

He took off his sunglasses and looked her in the eye with just a foot of space between them. His greasy veneer made her insides squirm with disgust, but she held her ground.

"That's all right. Let them have their fun first. I'll take over once they're done collecting evidence."

Samantha took a deep breath and found her courage.

She should be better than this. She shouldn't be afraid of standing her ground on a case.

But it was more than that. She wasn't afraid of standing up to Jordan. She was afraid of dropping the ball. A lifetime of not living up to people's ideas of who she should be and what she should be doing was taking up too much residence in her brain.

If she wanted to be the police chief of this town, though, she would have to get over that.

"Here's the thing," she said. "This is still my case."

A flicker of shock flashed across Jordan's face, then quickly disappeared as he chuckled. "Sam, honey, you lost this case the second you made that call. Because you couldn't handle things yourself."

That was bait.

She swallowed the rage boiling up at his *honey* and straightened her back. "I made that call because my job requires me to call your department whenever I have a potential murder investigation. We might need your crime lab, but we do not need your investigative services. I am still allowed to work *my* case."

This wasn't just some pissing contest to her, though. This was a victim in her town. Someone who should have been under her protection. She would do everything she could to find out what happened to Paul and make sure justice was served.

She doubted Jordan would give this case that kind of dedication.

He grinned. A slick grin, like the snake that he was. "At my discretion."

He wasn't wrong. But the fact that he would enjoy making her beg for the rights to her own dang case was one reason he had no business being chief. It was the reason she had to enter that race. The citizens of Etta deserved someone who put the town above their ego or some sick sense of competition.

"I know these people," she said.

"And they know you. Too well, maybe," he said. "Which is why outside folks should be on this."

Again, not wrong. But not entirely true either.

"These people aren't going to talk to your people like they'll talk to me," she said. "They'll be comfortable around me, and they'll give up information they wouldn't give to some outsider."

"Well, good thing I'm not an outsider." That disgusting grin widened.

She rarely wasted time hating people, but for Jordan Fonseca, she made an exception.

"I stand by my statement." She held his stare, this ridiculous game of glaring chicken taking place between them. "My town. My people. My case."

"How do I know you wouldn't feel sorry for someone or overlook them because they gave you a cookie one time when you were five?"

She opened her mouth to shut him down, but he held up a hand.

"I'm sorry, that was out of line."

An apology? From him?

Now Samantha was really suspicious. He'd had the authority to walk right in and kick her off of this thing. Off the property. Hell, he didn't even have to update her if he didn't want to. So why was he bothering to have this discussion?

"What do you want, Jordan?"

The grin disappeared, his mouth transforming into a gross pucker as he considered his words. "I want you busy. I want you so far out of your depth that this case eats you alive. I want you to fail. Hard."

The election. Of course.

He didn't care about anyone in Etta, much less about this victim or this case. He just wanted to win.

Samantha would have to prove to him and everyone else that she could handle both the race and the investigation. Maybe even win *because* she solved the case.

"Just stay out of my way."

One side of his mouth lifted in a smirk. "Not on your life, honey."

Erin paced the cement patio behind Zach's house while he drank a Coors Lite on the porch swing.

Movement helped with the shaking. Her hands had

been shaking ever since the reality set in that there had been a real freaking *dead man* in the bathroom with her.

After the short drive down the road in Zach's truck, Erin hadn't been sure if she would pass out or puke. One of those had seemed inevitable. But once Zach supplied a cold, wet rag for the back of her neck and settled her into a folding chair, both sensations subsided fairly quickly.

Too bad the shaking and the reality of her situation replaced the nausea and lightheadedness.

So she'd moved on to pacing.

Movement also helped her think. And she really needed to think of a way out of this.

"I don't see why this is such a big deal."

Erin shot Zach a glare, but continued her pacing.

"I mean, Paul, yeah. That's a big deal. Sure," he said. "But I don't get why it's such a big deal if you can't sell the house right away. It's not like it ain't paid off and costing you nothing."

"I need to get back to work."

"Then go," he said. "Can't you come take care of stuff when you need to?"

She could. On her days off. It was only an hour away from her apartment in New Orleans. But that back and forth would cost time and gas money. She wasn't exactly flush with either.

"I'm already taking time off to be here now. I don't have some fancy job with weeks of paid leave."

"I thought you were making jewelry or whatever. Can't you do that from anywhere?"

Technically, yes. In fact, she'd brought some inventory and supplies with her so she could fill orders while she was here. But that didn't pay all the bills. Not yet. "I also work part time at a store downtown."

Selling other people's jewelry and wishing it was hers. Her employer sold a few of her pieces on consignment, and she sold to a few other shops and set up tables at various festivals and events. But she couldn't do any of that around here. And she relied on that steady hourly pay. At least for now.

If she could only sell this house, she'd have a lot more options.

"I can't keep coming back to take care of this place," she continued. "Plus, there's Marty."

"I can look after the house," he said. "Hell, I already was."

"I appreciate it, but I can't ask you to do that indefinitely."

"It's no trouble, really," he insisted. "Your grandpa... well, you know how I felt about him. If I don't have your back, he'll probably come haunt me. And Marty likes me."

Erin wasn't sure Marty ever liked anyone but Grandpa, but Marty wasn't the point.

What was the point?

"I just want to get this all over with." Her voice cracked a little with that, and he looked at her with his big, sympathetic eyes.

She didn't want sympathy. From anyone.

He took a long, last drain of his beer, then nodded. "I get it."

Something in his eyes told her he really did understand. That maybe they shared more than a pair of deceased parents. That maybe they shared a similar desire to be free of this place. Someday. Somehow.

"But what can you do? You can't sell the place. I'll help however I can, but I can't make an open investigation go away."

Erin snapped her head up.

Zach just might be a freaking genius.

"That's it."

"What's it?"

"I make the case go away."

Zach scrunched his face. "How the hell you plan to do that?"

"We speed things along," she said. "We find out who murdered this guy and solve the case. Then the house is mine to sell, free and clear."

Zach's jaw went slack, then a second later he shook his head. "What's this we business?"

"You said you'd help however you could."

They stared at each other for a good long while, but Erin knew that look. She recognized that sparkle in his eye. She had him.

After a few more moments, he let out a low whistle. "Sam is *not* gonna like this."

Samantha.

Samantha with the dark, soulful eyes that made Erin's insides melt. Samantha with that wide smile Erin couldn't get enough of. Samantha with the tight pants and the BLT delivery service.

Samantha the fucking cop.

"Sam doesn't need to know about this."

"It's your funeral." Zach frowned. "And dang it, I've already been to one Sonnier funeral this month."

A stabbing pain seared through Erin's gut. She hadn't been able to bring herself here for the funeral. The whole town had shown up at the little church for her grandpa's last goodbye, and as far as they knew, she couldn't be bothered to show up.

What none of them knew was that she couldn't. Erin couldn't get out of bed that week. She'd cried in her pillow the whole day of the funeral and was in no condition to drive. She'd spent the week after his death in a haze of sedatives to keep herself in a calm depressive state instead of a hysterical fit.

So Erin had used up all her days off—unpaid, of course—crying over the loss of her grandpa and the guilt over not being there for his funeral. She couldn't waste any more time waiting around here to sell his house and all of his stuff.

She'd shed enough tears over this place and the last of the people she loved. There was nothing in this world left to upset her.

"Sam doesn't scare me."

Zach scoffed. "She scares me enough for both of us." He gave her a sideways glance. "There any particular reason she doesn't scare you?"

"No," she said, probably too quickly. "Besides, she's married. To an Ardoin at that."

"Was."

"Was what?"

"*Was* married," he clarified. "As in past tense. They divorced a couple years back."

"Oh."

Zach grinned.

"Wipe that off your face," Erin said. "I'm still not in the habit of actively crushing on potentially straight women. Or cops. Especially not that second one."

"A crush never hurt nobody."

Erin rolled her eyes and reeled the subject back in. "So you'll help me, right?"

"For the record," he said, "I don't like this plan. And you don't even know the first place to start looking for a murderer."

"That's why I've got *you* to help me. You can tell me everyone's stories."

He stared at her a bit longer, a deep frown set on his face, but they both knew she'd won already.

"Aw hell, why not."

Chapter Eight

SAMANTHA TAPPED the pencil eraser on the legal pad in front of her. At the top, she'd written "suspects" and underlined the word twice.

The rest of the page was blank.

Dustin walked by with a fresh mug of coffee and tapped a finger on the edge of her desk as he passed. "Want me to just print out a list of every known resident instead?"

She couldn't come up with a response, funny or otherwise. Her head was throbbing, her brain bouncing against the words of a certain deputy taking up unwelcome residency in her skull, and she had a town full of people her victim had pissed off.

"Might as well." She was normally optimistic at the beginning of any new investigation. After all, she'd never bumped up against a case she hadn't solved. Being completely stumped was unfamiliar territory for Samantha, and it was frustrating the heck out of her.

"All right," Dustin said in a chipper voice. The Pollyanna to her Eeyore. "Let's start easy. The usual suspects."

Samantha took a deep breath and sighed. "Fine."

"Romantic partner?"

They were both quiet, while a nearby Connie couldn't hold back a chuckle.

Paul had managed to annoy every person in this town at one time or another, so he'd long ago tainted his own stock as a potential romantic partner. Most people in town wouldn't speak to him, much less go out to dinner with him.

But people were mostly annoyed by his stray comments. Samantha couldn't remember anything serious enough to induce a fit of murderous rage or even vengeful payback.

He did have an ex-wife. They'd dated in high school, annoyed each other through twenty years of marriage, then got a quiet divorce, after which she moved to Florida with her sister. No one had seen her around Etta for several years, and Samantha couldn't think of a single reason she'd bother lifting a finger to kill Paul for.

"Okay, next," Dustin said. "Business partner?"

Paul had been a welder who worked alone out of his own backyard workshop. "Could be an irate customer." Samantha jotted that down at the bottom of her page.

"Fishing buddy?" Dustin asked.

Who on earth would kill someone over a recreational fishing dispute?

Only a handful of people were left in this town still

willing to even get in a car with Paul, let alone sit in a boat with the guy for half a day. She couldn't imagine any of them going through the trouble to kill Paul the way he died. They'd more likely just push him out of the boat.

Still, she jotted their names down, anyway. "Worth a look."

"Sibling?"

Samantha shook her head. His parents were both long gone from this world and his younger brother had gotten a football scholarship to Michigan State and never looked back. No one had seen him in years. Paul didn't even talk about him. And Paul did a *lot* of talking.

That could indicate some bad blood, but there was no inheritance or family land or anything for the brothers to fight over. By all accounts, they just didn't exist to each other anymore.

"Another relative?" Dustin frowned. "I know you don't want to hear this, but you've got to consider—"

"I know," she said, a little sharper than she'd intended. Truth was, she knew exactly who she had to put at the top of this list, but she didn't want to write the name down and look at it.

"You want me to talk to him instead?"

Yes. For the love of everything, yes, please.

"No, I should be the one to do it."

The guy was smart enough that he wouldn't slip up on anything he didn't want known to Dustin or her or anyone else. But if he had information that didn't incriminate him, she'd be the only one who could get it.

"I'll head over there later. I'm just seeing what other stops I need to make while I'm on the road." She tapped her pencil against the pad again. "Thing I can't figure is what Paul was doing in that house in the first place. Feels like that's the place to start, but I don't know where that is exactly."

Dustin studied her from across the room, thinking hard about those words. She hadn't expected him to figure out what she hadn't, but it was always enjoyable to watch him puzzle things out. He was turning out to be quite good at his job. If he wanted to, he could get a job in some bigger city one day. He'd probably end up making one heck of a detective.

"Think he just stumbled in drunk?" he asked.

Paul's truck had been found parked at his house near Addie's Lunch Shack. Not an impossible walk to Michael Sonnier's place, but a good enough distance for no one to have seen him stumbling on the side of the road or through a field to get there. And there wasn't even a bar between the two places.

"Could be a while on that tox screen and autopsy to know for sure." Samantha's brow furrowed as she considered a new possibility. "What if he went there with someone?"

"With the same someone who killed him?" Dustin looked intrigued but concerned by the possibility, mirroring Samantha's own internal turmoil over the implications.

"Maybe."

She didn't like where this train of thought was leading her. Didn't like it at all.

The door chimed and opened wide as a flustered, red-faced woman stormed into the station.

Samantha didn't like this turn of events, either.

She switched on her calm, professional officer voice and said, "Hello, Addie. What can we do for you?"

"You can start by telling me why that brute of a man set fire to my restaurant."

This was not how this day was supposed to go *at all*. This case was going to be hard enough in fifty different ways without Adeline stirring the pot with wild conspiracy mess and connecting dots that didn't exist.

But she knew there was no way to simply brush off Adeline, so she motioned to the chair beside her desk. "Have a seat, take a breath, and we'll talk. Officer Boutin, would you please get a cup of coffee for Mrs. Weaver?"

"Of course." Dustin rolled his eyes, but headed toward the coffeepot.

"Remind me, Adeline. How do you like your coffee?" she asked, her voice sweet as cane syrup now.

Addie sat in the chair and looked back and forth between the two officers, then stuttered slightly as she said, "Two sugars, lots of cream."

Samantha nodded at Dustin, who heard the order and nodded back. "Now, tell me why you think Paul was responsible for the fire at your restaurant. Because I know you believe it was intentional, but I've been over the files and statements again, and everything still points to an accident."

"Well, for starters, that man was practically the only person in town who didn't stick his nosy butt on my lot to see what happened."

Samantha listened quietly while Dustin placed Addie's coffee in front of her. She thanked him, and he smiled politely. Then, as he walked behind her, he twirled his finger beside his head with the universal cuckoo sign.

She made a mental note to talk to him later about showing respect for all of Etta's citizens, even the ones with wild conspiracy theories. Maybe especially those.

"I know that isn't a smoking gun or whatever you call it," Addie said, "but I heard from Justine that he parked himself in that gas station talking to her for over an hour while he watched my place burn."

Not a smoking gun. Not as far as Samantha saw it. Paul routinely "parked himself" in that gas station to harass Justine and anyone else who'd listen to him run his big obnoxious mouth.

"So why do you think Paul would have started a fire in your restaurant?"

From what Samantha could tell, there would have been no financial motive for anyone but Addie, least of all Paul. But since there hadn't been a murder in this town for as long as Samantha could remember, she doubted she'd stumbled upon some elaborate crime motivated by money. They were most likely looking at some sort of rage-fueled manslaughter case.

The needle prick in his neck, however, put a gigantic hole in that theory.

"That bastard hated me. Always has."

Samantha couldn't argue with that.

"But especially since I asked him to leave last month. Remember, I filed that report after he got handsy with one of my servers?"

Samantha did remember that. She also remembered that Paul didn't actually remember being kicked out because he'd been drunk that evening.

But the more Addie went on and on about Paul, the more firmly her grudges placed her on Samantha's suspect list. Even if it was more likely Addie would poison him in her restaurant than follow him to the Sonnier house to stick a needle in him. The best thing Samantha could do at this point was clear Addie *off* of that list.

"Addie, where were you yesterday afternoon?"

"Yesterday afternoon? Well, I was—" She flinched as her eyes widened with horror. "Samantha Keller Ardoin, are you accusing *me* of something? Because if there's anyone you should be questioning, it's that Erin girl. Happened in her house, and she *conveniently* found him. Not to mention she showed up in town at the exact time my restaurant burned, and a murder followed right behind. Downright suspicious, especially for someone who seems to always be in the thick of trouble, if you ask me."

Samantha shut her eyes tight and took a cleansing breath. She'd been trying and failing all morning not to think about Erin Sonnier. Not to call to see how she was doing. Not to go out there and—

"I need to know where you were yesterday," she repeated in a calm, clear voice. "I have to ask everyone."

Addie frowned with stern disapproval. She was clearly used to being the one doing the accusing. "I was at home. Making phone calls. Ordering a new fryer. Following up with insurance. Trying to figure out when I might be able to reopen."

"Can anyone verify that?"

"My insurance agent."

"Did you use your home phone or cell?" Samantha asked.

"My cell phone."

She'd really rather not have to get a court order to clear every single citizen in this town. So Samantha asked nicely, "Could we access your phone records to verify the calls and your location?"

Addie's frown settled in even deeper. "If it gets you on the way to finding out who killed that man before I could strangle him myself? Absolutely."

Erin placed her hands on the counter and whipped out her best smile. "Bet you didn't expect to see me again so soon."

The young man in a black polo shirt behind the clerk's office counter shook his head, but the hint of an amused smile played at the corner of his mouth. "Something told me I might see you around again before long.

You seem the kind that just can't stay out of the spotlight."

Erin's cheerful act faded as her shoulders dropped with a sigh. "Who've you been talking to?"

"You would be surprised how many people in this town have a story or two and can't wait to tell someone they think hasn't heard it before. You are quite the hot gossip topic around here."

Great. Absolutely nothing had changed.

Except this guy.

"How long did you say you've been here?" she asked sweetly.

"I didn't."

Erin rolled her eyes. She'd come here figuring she could pry some information out of the one person who was at least half as much an outsider in this place as she was, simply by the fact of being an actual outsider not born and raised in this hellhole. Turned out he was way smarter than everyone else around there and not at all fooled by her act.

"Five years," he said anyway. "We moved here my senior year."

She'd been close, guessing his age. "Long enough to listen and know things, but not long enough to feel some sense of loyal obligation to the good folks of Etta?"

"Something like that." He leaned toward her over the counter. "Since when did you join the Etta Police Department? Should I be calling you Detective Erin?"

"Not on your life." Or anyone else's. Being a cop would be her nightmare. Not to mention it would compromise every one of the few moral sticking points she had.

Being pressed up against a cop, however—especially a certain Etta sergeant who'd specifically suggested that Erin lay low for a while...

"I'm just a concerned citizen."

"A concerned citizen with a history of petty arson and the proud new owner of a homicide crime scene?"

This guy was too damn smart. Well, too smart and smug for her own personal purposes at the moment. His smartass attitude would probably serve him well in life. And her current needs and circumstance aside, she kind of liked the guy.

"Alleged petty arson," she corrected.

"My mistake." His smug smirk grew wider. "So what can I do for the notorious criminal mastermind of the great town of Etta today?"

"I need information."

"I gave you all the forms you needed yesterday."

"People information," she said. "Tips on who might have left a dead guy in my house."

"Thought you weren't a detective?"

"I'm just someone who can't leave this godforsaken place behind permanently until I sell that house. And I can't sell that house until it isn't a key location in an active murder case any longer. I thought *maybe* you'd be someone who might understand my desire to get the hell out of here and be willing to point me in the right direction."

"You sure are making a lot of assumptions about

me." He narrowed his dark eyes at her. "Least of which is what makes you think I know anything useful?"

"You already slipped and told me you're the recipient of all the hot gossip about me. I'm sure people have run their mouths to you about all sorts of things. Whatever your story is, you still have a natural charisma. People can't help themselves. They talk, so you know things."

He thought for a moment, then clearly decided not to argue against her logic. "What's in it for me?"

"The satisfaction of helping?"

He didn't respond, only frowned and raised his brow.

"Fine. What do you want?"

He thought for another moment. "A favor."

"What favor?"

"I don't know yet. Let's just say you owe me one."

"Ugh, fine," she said. "I, Erin Sonnier, owe you..."

"Trey."

"I, Erin Sonnier, owe you, Trey, a future favor of your choosing."

With any luck at all, she'd be long gone before he came to collect on that.

"Good," he said. "Now, what do you want to know?"

Erin chewed on the inside of her mouth, thinking about where to start. Finally, she said, "Tell me everyone who hated Paul Latiolais."

Trey laughed. "How much time have you got?"

Chapter Nine

SAMANTHA KNOCKED ON THE DOOR. Three quick raps. She straightened her back and shoulders to stand tall, attempting to project more confidence than she had at that moment.

The crepe myrtles flanking the driveway were still in full bloom, their pink petals blanketing the front lawn. She'd always loved those trees. Loved seeing them out the window from the reading chair on steamy summer afternoons when it was too hot to sit out on the porch if there wasn't a breeze.

The door opened, snapping Samantha's attention back. Her ex stood in the doorway. Relaxed and composed. His classic good looks were as physically attractive as ever.

Beneath the physical veneer, however, was a swamp of ugly Samantha knew all too well.

"I was wondering when you'd show up," he said.

"Sooner than I'd imagined. Getting better at the whole sergeanting thing, huh?"

Why must every man in her life insist on baiting her?

"Good to see you too, Nathan."

It was not at all good to see Nathan Ardoin.

As much as she loved her job working in a small town—knowing the ins and outs of everyone's lives and interacting with the citizens—she hated regularly brushing up against people she'd booted from her personal life. If she could go the rest of her days without ever seeing her ex-husband again, she'd be a very happy woman.

Nathan, thankfully, decided not to play around and waste her time any more than he had while they'd been married.

"I didn't kill him."

She stood at a loss for words, staring at the man she'd once foolishly loved. The man who now made her skin crawl.

He'd always been blunt, especially with her, but he was also a master manipulator. For him to jump to the point without dancing around the truth meant he didn't want her sniffing at something.

"Don't look so shocked," he said. "That *is* why you're here, isn't it?"

She ignored the condescension and dismissal in his voice. Or tried to, at least. "May I come in? I do have a few questions for you that aren't answered with that one statement."

The words burned like acid. She was asking this man

to enter the house she'd once lived in. The house she'd called her own home for five years.

Now she was standing at the front door, begging for an invitation.

She hated it, but she wouldn't go through her questions in the doorway. He had the upper hand at the moment. She needed to either get control of their interaction or at least get on equal footing.

He paused longer than necessary, just to piss her off or make her uncomfortable. Maybe both.

Then he moved aside and gestured. "Of course."

"Thank you."

Samantha took a deep breath and stepped through the entryway. The place still looked exactly the same. Same furniture she'd picked out. Same books on the shelves. *Her* books on the shelves. It was all the same as the day she'd left. If it were anyone else, she'd assume he was too lazy or too busy or too unconcerned to change things and make the place his own after the divorce. But since this was Nathan, she knew the truth: he'd used her.

He'd taken her free labor in researching and purchasing and designing the place, and he'd claimed her work as his own. Like he did with everyone and everything he touched. He absorbed the people and things around him, building the facade of a life and personality from the people he chewed up and spit out, like some grotesque sci-fi creature.

Not that she'd had much of an identity on her own before him. She'd always been her mother's daughter, then she was Nathan's wife. It didn't matter that she had her own name or job or life. To everyone else, she was just "a Keller" and then "an Ardoin."

Now, she was finally just Samantha.

Not that her first name held any weight on its own or that anyone cared about it. But she felt good to be her own person finally.

Even if she was still carrying around the weight of that last name.

He followed her into the living room and sat in the dark blue wingback chair he knew she loved. With her jaw set so firmly she'd have to take ibuprofen that night to ease the inflammation, Samantha sat on the edge of the nearby loveseat.

She put her legal pad in her lap and clicked open her pen. "I'm just here to ask a few questions. As you can imagine, I'll be asking a lot of people questions over the next couple days. You are not my lead suspect in Paul's death, but I do need to clear some things up to eliminate you."

If only she could legally eliminate him from her life for good.

He gave his smarmy smile and tapped the arm of the chair with his fingertips. "You've gotten better at this."

Definitely ibuprofen later.

"Let's start with the obvious," she said. "Where were you yesterday afternoon?"

He gave another sly smile. "With a friend."

"I'm going to assume your vague answer means it was a female friend." Her stomach rolled, but not from any lingering jealousy or hurt. Her nausea was from pure disgust. "Name."

"It's... a delicate matter."

"So she's married. Got it. Can she confirm that you were with her yesterday afternoon?"

"She can," Nathan said. "Whether she will or not is up to her, not me."

Samantha frowned. "Please don't make this harder than it needs to be. For either of us."

She knew he didn't give a rat's ass about making things easier for her any more than Deputy Fonseca wanted to make things easier for her. But she also knew he'd want to make things easier for himself. He *always* wanted that. It was usually his entire M.O.

"When was the last time you spoke to Paul?"

He tilted his head to give her a downward look and raised his brow. "What year is it?"

"I'm serious, Nathan."

"So am I. That cretin and I had no reason to speak to one another. If you could even call all the grunting he did 'speech.'"

Ever the elitist.

If she hadn't had to bear much of his derision herself, she might have been inclined to cut him some slack. Her ex-husband came from a long line of folks who thought they were better than everyone else. And not just better than the citizens of Etta. Better than everyone. Every-where. Always. They were big, ugly fish who were completely unaware of the size of their tiny pond.

And they'd done a bang-up job training their offspring to believe that nonsense.

Case in point.

She regretted a lot about her marriage to Nathan Ardoin, but one thing she would never regret was leaving without adding any children to that family. No heirs of hers they could ever attempt to brainwash.

"Paul isn't the one being questioned here today. You are."

"But shouldn't he?" He leaned back in his chair. "After all, he was trespassing himself, I hear."

"Any idea why Paul might have been there?"

"Why would I know that? I told you I haven't spoken to the man."

They might not have spoken, but Paul did a lot of talking *about* Nathan. The whole town knew Paul's beef with him. Legitimate or not. He'd gotten hooked on pain pills and blamed Nathan's pharmacy as much as the doctor for his addiction and depleted bank account. Nathan had more cause than anyone she could think of to shut Paul up for good.

"But you hear things. And you know things. You're a smart man." It was her turn to give a sly smile as she gestured at the bookcases beside her. "I mean, you have all these books."

His eyes narrowed, an uncharacteristic flash of untempered rage in them. A charlatan's greatest fear was being unmasked.

"I'm afraid the motivations of Paul Latiolais are beyond my scope of reference."

"So you haven't heard anything about why he might have been at that house? What he might have been doing there or looking for or who he might have been with?"

A curious twitch hit his lip. "What makes you think he was with someone?"

"I can't reveal the details of an open case."

Which also meant she couldn't reveal about the needle or why that made him look like a prime suspect. Nathan had inherited his family's pharmacy. *The* pharmacy in Etta. Word was they owned a few doctors, too. Nathan would have had easy access to whatever would come back from the autopsy and tox screen reports.

It was also a Nathan kind of crime. Clean. No mess.

She didn't think for a second that he'd get his own hands dirty, even like this, but she could believe he'd pay someone else to make a problem go away. She was living proof of that.

Any jury in the world would take one quick look at his history and believe he was capable of paying for a hit. He'd made plenty of people go away with cash. Just hadn't escalated to permanently-go-away levels before now.

Nathan leaned over the chair arm and reached to place a hand on hers. "Sam, do you think maybe this case is a little... big for you?"

She pulled her hand away and tried to keep her eyes steady. Tried to keep them from turning into pits of flaming rage lava. Tried to keep from showing that he'd gotten to her.

"I have backing from the parish and the state," she said. "*If* I need them."

Not that he was worried about her. He was just trying to get under her skin. Rattle her. Like all the men threatened by the possibility of her actually being good at her job.

He leaned back in his chair again and smiled. "Good. I'm glad you have help. Speaking of help." His head tilted in curiosity. "Where's that cheerful little lap dog of yours today?"

She knew exactly what he meant, but she replied, "Dexter is at home, where he always is."

"I meant your protégé. Officer... what was his name again?"

"Officer Boutin is on call at the station today."

"Seems to me y'all pay him far too much to smile and fetch coffee."

This current iteration of his smile set the hairs on the back of Samantha's neck to stand at attention.

Nathan was hiding something. And he was toying with her.

Whether he knew something related to the case or whether this was simple reputation preservation, she couldn't tell. What she did know was that he wouldn't reveal anything unless he wanted to. And she didn't have any leverage for digging further.

Yet.

"I'm going to need to confirm your whereabouts yesterday. Tell me who you were with."

His smile faded to a slight grimace. He wasn't used to her being this direct or to him being the one on defense.

"I'd rather not."

"I'm sure you'd rather not be a prime suspect with no alibi even more." It was her turn to smile.

Leverage.

She didn't have an ounce of it when they'd been married or during the divorce. It felt good to finally have the upper hand on her ex. Too bad it took a man's death to get it.

"I'll need you to promise discretion."

She didn't owe him a damn thing, and smearing him would bring her so much joy. But she needed the name of whoever this woman was. Someone who most likely didn't deserve Samantha's wrath or retribution. "Fine. I'll do what I can. *Name*."

He frowned as she relished his displeasure, wishing she could make the weasel squirm even more.

After considering his options, he said, "Rhea."

Samantha ran through her mental list of every Etta citizen she could remember. There was only one Rhea on that list. But Nathan couldn't be that careless.

Could he?

"Last name."

He was silent for a long moment, then a crack appeared in Nathan's confident veneer as he said, "Rhea Blanchard."

83

Chapter Ten

ERIN PUT MORE money in her parking meter, then walked back down Main Street toward the little cafe Trey had agreed to meet her at if she bought him lunch. With some time before Trey's work break, Erin decided to snoop around a bit while she waited for him.

Main Street was a three-block strip of stores and government buildings, including the clerk's office and the police station at the far end of the street. Not much had changed. Same shops, only she noticed as she walked past Mr. Robicheaux's place that he had a display pot outside filled with metal irises on stakes. She smiled at the pretty decorations, something she wouldn't have expected from the gruff man she remembered.

A little farther down, she saw what appeared to be the only empty store space downtown. It was narrow but had big front windows like all the other shops. A perfect spot for a boutique, maybe something similar to the one back home where she sold her jewelry on consignment.

Back home... in New Orleans.

It felt so strange to be here again. This was no longer her home, but it still had an odd familiar tug at her soul, even after all these years.

She walked a little more, then circled back to the cafe where she was meeting Trey. It wasn't until she saw the name on the glass door that she realized this was the same place Samantha had picked up her sandwich from less than two days ago. Her heart raced as she stared at the outside of the cafe door.

Her phone rang in her bag to snap her out of her fluster.

"Hey, Zach."

"Between dog walks and just checking on how your sleuthing is going."

Erin felt a warm sensation run through her. She wasn't used to anyone checking on her. Heck, none of her New Orleans friends had checked on her in three days. They'd barely spared the breath to tell her they were sorry about her grandfather. Even her roommate hadn't really cared. In all fairness, they hardly ever spoke to each other, only exchanging polite small talk between his night shifts at the hospital.

But Zach, who she hadn't seen or spoken to in years, had called to see how she was doing mere hours after she'd last seen him. He'd even offered his spare room when Erin had a mild panic attack over the thought of going back to her own house last night. She considered herself pretty tough, but finding a dead guy in her bathroom apparently surpassed her toughness limit.

So she'd taken him up on his offer, popped a sedative, and slept through the night, sneaking out early this morning before he'd woken up for work at the vet clinic.

"Good so far," she lied.

In truth, she had next to nothing. All her hopes for an early exit from Etta hinged on Trey having some juicy gossip that might actually be useful. "I'm meeting a new friend for lunch to try and get the scoop on some of the Main Street folks."

After a long pause, Zach asked, with a hint of confusion in his voice, "A new friend?"

She almost felt guilty, like she was friend-cheating on Zach. Being back here was making her feel all sorts of weirdness.

But his confusion was warranted. She hadn't really had any friends when she lived here. It did sound odd to say she had a new one in a mere two days of being back. If anyone knew how bad she was at friendship, it was Zach.

"Sort of." Trey wasn't an actual friend, but she didn't know what else to call him. "Someone I met yesterday while taking care of paperwork."

"Been in town less than three days and you've already made a new friend you're gossiping over lunch with?" After another pause, Zach laughed. "Who are you? Where's Erin? And what did you do with her?"

"Don't worry, I'm not replacing you. You're my bird guy. And my friend for when I find a murder victim in my house."

"Leave it to you to need that kind of friend," he said.

"So who's this new person, and what kind of scoop you hoping to get out of 'em?"

"His name's Trey. He works at the Clerk's office. Do you know him?"

"Erin, everyone knows everyone here."

"Right, but you know what I mean."

"Yeah, I know him. Transferred from somewhere a few years after we graduated. Seems okay, I guess." After a brief pause, Zach added, "Don't really know much but that he got in a bad accident or something right about after they got here."

"What kind of accident?"

"Car. Went to the hospital a while. There was... talk."

"Talk?"

"You know how that goes."

Erin did know how that went. Lots of words flying around town, very little of them true.

"People said he had problems, but hell if I know what's real or not," Zach said. "Anyway, keeps to himself and helps out with his parents mostly."

"Well, apparently the Clerk's office is gossip central, so he's going to fill me in on some town stuff. Hopefully." She spotted Trey walking toward her. "He's here. I've gotta go. Thanks for checking in on me."

"Sure thing," he said. "Guest room is open if you're still freaked out later."

"Thanks. Really, I mean it. Talk to you later."

She ended the call just as Trey approached and held the cafe door open for her.

"Thanks," she said. "I'd forgotten how much everyone here is into the whole chivalry thing."

"It's more courtesy than chivalry. And a bit of a reflex now. I'm pretty sure my mom would pop up from around a random corner if she caught me not holding a door for someone."

"Your mom is still here in town?"

"Yeah." He gestured for Erin to pick a table. Lots of options as the lunch rush was clearing out. "She and my dad became ride or die for this town. They both love the horses and cane fields and fresh air. Mom works at the parish hospital, and Dad opened a mechanic shop on the property."

"Out of curiosity, why are *you* still here? Most people I went to school with got out or got stuck."

They took seats across from each other at a small table.

"I had some health issues," Trey said. "So I guess I'm in the got stuck group. I'm taking online classes. Maybe one day I'll change groups."

The server placed two menus and two glasses of water in front of them.

"What are you studying?"

"Library science."

"Huh," she said with mild amusement. "I didn't peg you for the librarian type."

"Books kept me sane most of my childhood. Gave me hope and all that, no matter where we were." He shrugged. "Now I want to get the right books in kids' hands. Let every kid see themselves and a way out.

Stock shelves for all kinds of kids... especially queer kids."

She definitely respected that. But it took an extra second for the implication at the end of his statement to sink in. "Oh!"

He chuckled softly. "Keep it low."

"Sure. Of course."

"Your reputation preceding you and all, I figured you'd be cool knowing."

"Yeah, that's one reputation that's actually accurate," she said. "Thanks for sharing that. Your secret is safe with me as long as you want it to stay that way."

"Thanks." He hesitated, then said, "I've got enough red flags pinned to me for now. Not that it *should* be a red flag, but I'm tired of proving myself to people. Besides, no one needs to know my business unless I want them to."

"That's fair." She wanted to know what red flags he was referring to, but she didn't want to pry too much yet. She knew it couldn't be easy being a black man in a small town, much less a queer black man, but she got the feeling he was referencing something else.

"How much have you heard about me?" he asked.

"I don't know if you've noticed, but I don't have a whole lot of pals to hear things from."

He laughed. "I'm serious."

With a shrug, she said, "Zach heard you were in some kind of accident a while back. Said you maybe went to the hospital and there was gossip, but he knows as well as I do not to put much stock in any of that."

"I have a feeling some of the rumors about *you* are true, though," he said with a sly grin.

"Oh, definitely."

He laughed again. It was a deep, relaxed laugh. One she got the impression he didn't let out very often.

"So you know how I said earlier that I had some health issues?" When she nodded, he said, "The accident Zach mentioned was my first manic episode. I don't know how fast I was going, but I flipped the car. Thankfully, I didn't hurt anyone else and was just banged up a bit myself. That hospital stay was inpatient at a mental hospital."

"Oh. Wow. I'm glad you were okay." She scrambled to find the right words to say next. She didn't want to come across like an asshole, but she wasn't usually great at not coming across that way. "For the record, I don't think having a mental illness is a red flag at all. Not even a yellow one."

"Thanks." Trey let out a grunt and said, "Tell that to the rest of the world."

"People around here seem to like you."

"That's because I try not to burn shit down."

Erin shook her head and laughed. Somehow, she didn't mind Trey poking at her well-earned reputation. "Fair enough. So that's why you stuck around?"

"It took a while to find the right meds and get my feet under me again after that." He picked at the edge of his menu. "Samantha was the first person at the accident. She could have filed charges or some shit after I got cleaned up, but I guess she recognized I needed help. She called my mom, and they both got me admitted to the hospital. If that had happened anywhere else, I probably wouldn't have been so lucky."

"Yeah, I can imagine that could have been even worse for you."

It was his turn to shrug. "Anyway, I figured I'd clear that up before you heard some wild tale about what happened."

"Again, thanks for sharing that with me." She wasn't sure why, but it warmed her that he did. "People don't usually trust me with anything."

The server returned and took their orders. A tuna melt for Trey, and a BLT for Erin. The one Samantha had brought her the other night had been good. Worth a repeat. Even if it wasn't quite Addie's level of good.

"For the record," Trey said, "you're buying. And this isn't the favor you owe me."

"Noted."

"What specifically do you want to know?"

"Let's start with Paul, since I don't really remember him or anyone he hung around with."

"Probably because Paul used to be a decent guy, from what I understand. Worked offshore. Didn't cause much trouble. Went fishing a lot when he was home."

"He was talking about fishing when I ran into him." She recalled the conversation she'd walked in on at the gas station. "I'm guessing his fishing buddy probably wanted to push him over the side more than once, based on what I heard."

"Yup. That would be Richard Cole. They had the

bitchiest friendship I've ever seen. But yeah, I'm guessing if Richard got that mad, he'd just push Paul out of the boat and drive off, like you said."

"So probably not Richard. Got it." She nodded. "If Paul used to be such a decent guy, what happened?"

Trey frowned. "Rig accident. Pretty bad. Couldn't work anymore, but got worker's comp. From what I've pieced together, he got hooked on pain meds. No one around here reads a damn label, and not a doctor or pharmacist warned him. Just kept prescribing and filling those prescriptions, increasing the dose when Paul said they weren't working instead of getting him on something better."

"Ardoin's Pharmacy?" It was such a common last name that Erin had forgotten it happened to belong to the wealthiest family in Etta.

"That would be the one, since it's the only one."

"Wait a minute..." The pharmacy name flashed a memory of that badge in her mind. She'd been so enamored with that smile and those tight pants that she hadn't put two and two together the other day. "Sam married *the* Ardoins?"

Trey nodded. "Nathan Ardoin."

"Oh. Ew."

"Yup. That's pretty much what everyone thought. The guy is straight-up hot garbage."

She remembered Nathan hanging around school events even though he'd graduated. Definitely creepy vibes. She wondered what the hell Samantha saw in that guy. She always came across as very sensible. But in a no-bullshit way, not in a ladder-climbing way. Certainly never seemed the type to be impressed by another family's money and prestige, especially since her own family had its own wealth and power. She didn't need Nathan for that, even if she had been under his money's spell.

"So Nathan's pharmacy and some shady-ass doctor got Paul hooked and basically ruined his life. Sounds like motive."

"Yeah, but motive for Paul, if anyone."

Erin considered that. "Maybe Paul was going to reveal that they were over-prescribing?"

"Did he seem like the investigative type to you? Or at least that he might be successful at it?"

"Maybe he stumbled onto something else?" Although she couldn't think of anything that would have had him stumbling into her grandpa's house.

Trey thought for a moment, then nodded. "Stumbling was definitely a Paul kind of thing."

The server placed their sandwiches in front of them and asked if they needed anything else. When they thanked her, Trey dove into his tuna melt while Erin crunched on a ruffled chip and continued to ponder this potential theory.

"The pharmacy also gives Nathan access to whatever might have killed Paul."

Trey chewed his massive bite and swallowed. "You think Nathan would kill someone?"

"I don't really know the guy." She waved her half-eaten chip in the air. "But we can't dismiss him. Because with his connection to the police, they might."

Trey grunted. "I doubt Sergeant Ardoin would let him get away with jaywalking if she could bust him with it. That marriage did not end pleasantly."

Erin popped the chip in her mouth to keep from asking questions that had nothing to do with the murder.

Trey eyed her curiously, then a playful smile formed.

She decided to play ignorant as a deflection tactic and pretend she hadn't already had this conversation with Zach. "I just assumed she was still married with the last name and all."

"People know her by that name, so I guess it made sense to keep it. Especially now with the election and all. Although hanging on to that of all names can't be fun."

"No, I guess not." Erin tried to imagine walking around with a name that was not only not yours, but one that had so much baggage attached to it.

They both ate in silence, with Trey nearly finished his lunch already. Erin's was tasty, but she wasn't very hungry anymore.

"Aside from Nathan, anyone else around here ring alarm bells?"

"Everyone was low-key annoyed by Paul," Trey said. "But no one I can think of would go out of their way to kill the guy."

"What about anyone who seems shady? Anyone with legal trouble? Even small stuff they got away with?"

"Besides you and me?"

Erin narrowed her eyes at him, but couldn't stop

herself from smiling back once she saw the teasing grin on Trey's face.

He thought for a second while he finished off the last of his sandwich.

"The only person I can really think of like that doesn't have much of an actual record. In trouble a lot, but somehow slides out of it."

"How's that?"

"Last name is Keller."

Sam's maiden name.

Erin remembered Samantha having a sister, Melanie, and a clean-as-a-whistle goody-two-shoes brother, but neither of them would dare step out of line for fear of inviting the wrath of their mother. The extended family, however, was an amorphous blob of political yuck.

"A cousin?"

"Yeah, younger," Trey said. "Probably graduated after you, but before I got here."

Samantha was going to have her hands full between her dirtbag ex and her own family mess.

"Got a name? What does he do around here besides get into trouble?"

"Randy," Trey said. "He works in the kitchen at Addie's on and off. Does roofing jobs sometimes."

"Gotcha." Erin etched the name into her memory. "Anyone else? Anyone Paul might have had beef with? Even petty?"

"One person." Trey shook his head in disbelief. "But we'll have to talk about that later."

"Later? Why?"

He nodded toward the door as he held up his next chip. "Because she just walked in. And I'm pretty sure she's headed this way to accuse *you* of something."

Erin was confused for only about half a second. Then she heard that voice behind her. The one she could never in a million years forget. The one she'd been avoiding since she'd stepped foot back in this town.

The voice abruptly stopped rambling to the cashier and said, "Give me one minute. I see someone I need to have a chat with."

Chapter Eleven

ERIN SLUMPED IN HER CHAIR.

"Crap."

"Mmhmm," Trey murmured over his chip crunching. He swallowed, then forcefully brightened his expression and sat up straight. "How are you, Mrs. Weaver?"

Adeline Weaver stood over them, looking back and forth between Trey and Erin. "I didn't know you two were acquainted."

Erin forced a smile that felt more like a dry-rotted rubber band about to snap. "Hello, Addie. Good to see you."

"I've been helping Erin with her grandfather's estate and final business affairs."

Trey's smile was much more natural than Erin's. His effortless display of charisma was impressive. And probably handy now that she knew his history and how everyone around here must have initially reacted around him. Charm could be a very useful survival tool.

Addie's expression shifted from prepared-to-pounce to ready-to-bake-a-sympathy-cake.

She turned her attention to Erin. "I haven't had the chance to tell you how sorry I was to hear about his passing. You must be devastated. We all feel his loss very deeply around here."

"Thank you, Addie," Erin said. "It's been... hard."

Her throat threatened to close up just saying those words. It was harder than she'd ever imagined, yet she didn't want to let anyone know how hard. And she sure as hell didn't want to talk about it. Especially not with Addie.

"I'm sure it has been, dear." Her voice dropped. "I thought I'd heard talk that you were back in town, but I was so busy that day. What with the *fire* and all."

So much for any lasting effects from Trey's charm.

The bells on the cafe door jingled as someone new entered the restaurant, but Erin didn't dare take her eyes off the woman staring her down.

"Yes, I heard about your loss, too. I'm so sorry." She forced another smile and tried to channel some of that Trey magic. "Your BLT was the first thing I came looking for when I got here."

The woman's cheeks brightened at the compliment, but she wasn't deterred from her goal. "Strange how my kitchen caught on fire the same day you rolled into town, isn't it?"

Trey cleared his throat and shifted in his seat. He seemed to raise his brow at someone across the room behind her, but Erin had her hands full at the moment and couldn't see who was at the diner door.

"That is quite the coincidence," Erin acknowledged, refusing to take Addie's bait.

"Coincidence? Young lady—"

"Well, hello, Mrs. Weaver!" Sam's voice cut through the conversation with out-of-character enthusiasm and a big, bold grin. "Trey. Erin. Good to see everyone."

"Hello there, Sergeant Ardoin." Trey made an exaggerated grimace at her while Addie's attention was torn between Samantha and Erin.

Samantha was clearly alert to the trouble already, although Erin could have handled Addie on her own. She'd had enough of the woman's derision to know she was all bluster and bark, but had no real bite to speak of. Like pretty much everyone else around here.

Still, if she didn't have to be the one to deal with it today, all the better.

The bonus was the tingle of heat creeping up the back of Erin's neck at the sight of Samantha. Her cheeks were probably turning red with heat as well. Hopefully, she hadn't imagined that tiny glimmer of mutual interest the other night. Maybe Erin could even forget that Samantha was a cop... temporarily, that is.

"Samantha, I was just telling Erin that it is quite strange that she showed up here just as—"

"Actually, Mrs. Weaver, I was wondering if I could speak with you about something important. Would you mind chatting with me for a second over here while I wait for my to-go order?"

Addie flinched and looked back and forth between Erin and Samantha. "Well, if it's important, I suppose so."

Samantha guided Addie back toward the front counter. With a wink over her shoulder, she said, "Y'all enjoy the rest of your lunch. Good to see you."

Erin didn't like the idea of Addie spouting off lies and crackpot theories about her in Samantha's ear. Not one bit. But she'd spent enough years defending herself around here. She'd take any break she could get from that Weaver wrath.

"Soooooooo." It sounded like Trey could drag that word out for a whole week. He wagged his eyebrows at her with a quick glance toward the front counter. "Sergeant Ardoin, huh? I'm not a big fan of the policing system as a whole, as I know you must not be either." There was that sly grin again. "But with Sam... I don't know. I could maybe see it for you."

Erin felt her cheeks flush even hotter as she grabbed a chip from her plate and tossed it at Trey's pile. "Isn't your lunch break over soon?"

"I'm telling you, that is too much of a coincidence," Addie said, wagging a finger in the air. "That girl showing up here the same day as my fire? She was already responsible for one, now mine. How many more's she got in store for us?"

The last thing Samantha had time for this week was

defending Erin Sonnier to Addie, but she couldn't very well let the woman eat Erin for lunch.

"Erin had nothing to do with what happened to your restaurant. She wasn't even in town yet when it started."

"How do you know that? For all you know—"

"I know because I stopped her outside your place while you were talking to the insurance people," Samantha said. "She'd just gotten into town and was looking for dinner. I had to explain what happened."

Addie grunted. "She could have been lying. How do you know she was telling you the truth? Could have been snooping around to see the results of her handiwork."

"Justine saw her in the gas station first. She'd just come in to fill up. Paul saw her, too."

"She could have been fibbing to them." Addie's shoulders sagged. "And poor Paul. Don't you think there are just too many coincidences?"

She should have let it go, but Samantha couldn't allow this ridiculous thought train to roll on any further. "You can't possibly be suggesting Erin had anything to do with Paul's death."

"Well, she did find him. In her own house."

"I assure you I will look into every possible lead, but I honestly do not believe Erin had anything to do with that homicide." Samantha crossed her arms. "And since when is he poor Paul? You've been ready to strangle him yourself for as long as I can remember."

"Yes, but I didn't want the man to *die*."

Fair enough.

Samantha glanced at Erin and Trey finishing their

lunches. It was a good sight, the both of them laughing. She was glad they'd found their way to each other.

Trey was doing well, as far as Samantha knew from chatting and checking in with his mom from time to time. But it had been hard for him to make and keep friends. People around here liked him well enough, but they still kept him at arm's length.

As for Erin, Samantha was glad any time she saw her smile. Even when Samantha wasn't the reason for it.

When she returned her attention to Addie, she found the woman giving her a curious look.

"What?"

"I need to get back to the restaurant." Addie handed her credit card to the cashier in exchange for two over-flowing plastic bags. "Just picking up sandwiches for my crew. They're working hard to help get the place back up and running."

Leave it to Addie. Stirring up trouble for one person while feeding her employees and giving business to her competition. The woman was a whole mess of mixed signals.

"I hope everything goes smoothly and you're back up and running soon."

"Thank you." Addie put a hand on Samantha's forearm. "And I do hope you find whoever killed Paul. I'll help you bury the son of a somebody who did it myself."

Samantha gave her an appreciative smile and held the door as Addie left with her bags and one last over-the-shoulder glance at the table near the back of the cafe.

The second the door closed behind her, Erin and Trey stood and headed toward Samantha.

"Thanks for that," said Erin.

She looked dimmer. For all her misery in this place, Erin had always had this colorful aura, like she was a walking box of crayons. But that color was faded now. The loss of her grandfather, finding a dead man in her bathroom, and being hounded by Addie were apparently draining the life from her.

"No problem," Samantha said. "Addie can be a lot. But she's good people."

"If you say so."

Trey cleared his throat. "Lunch break's over. I'll see you two later. Good luck!"

Samantha had a sinking suspicion that was meant for Erin, and she wasn't sure what Erin might need luck with. She was even less sure she wanted to know.

Great, now she sounded paranoid like Addie.

The server handed Samantha her to-go order, which she paid for with cash.

"On a late lunch break yourself?" Erin asked.

"Just finished some interviews and grabbing something to eat back at the station."

"Any luck with the investigation?"

"It's still early," Samantha said. "I have a lot of things to look into."

She'd hoped to get more out of Nathan, and now she would have to check out his alibi. Discreetly. She was half-tempted to rat him out and let the woman's jealous husband have at him. But she had more integrity than that.

"I'm actually parked down by the station."

"We can walk that way together." Samantha tried not to sound as delighted as she was by this tiny turn of events. It was just a block.

Sheesh. She was acting like a giddy teenager.

"Who'd you interview this morning? Can you tell me?"

"I probably shouldn't, but we both know how this town works, so you'll hear everything soon enough." Samantha took a big inhale before saying his name. "I started with Nathan. My ex-husband."

"So it's true?" Erin said. "You really married that sleazeball?"

"Not one of my better life decisions, but yeah. I did."

Hardly a day went by that she didn't regret the years she'd wasted on that man. She could forgive herself for falling for his initial charm—she'd been so young and naive—but she couldn't forgive herself for not having the courage to walk away sooner, when she knew things were bad and would never get better.

Erin shrugged, her turquoise bob bouncing with the motion. "We've all got our regrets." She gave a sideways smile. "At least yours didn't get you a reputation for arson."

Samantha held up a finger. "*Alleged* arson."

Erin laughed. "Oh, I burned that shit."

Samantha covered her ears. "I cannot hear this."

"Only regret was not burning that shed with the jerk

in it." Erin sighed. "No, that's a lie. I regret the trouble I made for Grandpa."

"He knew you loved him. And he'd have defended you against any angry pitchfork mob any day of the week." Her heart broke for Erin. Everyone knew that if they wanted to get to Erin, they'd have to go through Michael Sonnier, and no one would risk that. Gentlest man you'd ever meet, but he was fierce as a honey badger for his granddaughter. Samantha couldn't imagine the pain of his loss, and she wanted to wrap her arms around Erin and hold her right there on Main Street.

"This is my car," Erin said, digging for her keys in her bag. "I guess I'll see you around."

Samantha froze and stared in front of her, not believing what she was looking at. "Um, you aren't going anywhere."

Erin eyed Samantha cautiously. "Am I in some kind of trouble? I already gave my statement."

"No," Samantha said quickly. "Well, a little, but not legal."

Erin's face scrunched in an adorable way that made the tip of her nose lift slightly. "What kind of trouble, then?"

Samantha pointed to the front of Erin's car, where the driver's side tire was completely flattened beside the curb.

"Probably hit a nail on the way in. They replaced the roof on one of these buildings not long ago. I can get Frank to come patch that right here for you. His shop's not far around the corner." Samantha checked the time on the big bank clock down the road. "But it might be a bit. Can I give you a ride? He can drive the car back to your place when it's done."

Erin frowned deeply at the tire. She sighed and pulled out her phone. "Thanks, but I think I can get a ride."

"Are you sure?"

"Yeah." Erin pointed at the bag in Samantha's hand and pushed out a tiny half-smile. "You should eat."

Erin typed out a quick text, while Samantha waited to make sure she had a ride home. She was definitely the type to brush off help and insist she could take care of herself. Samantha didn't doubt that she probably could, but Addie's little confrontation was just the tip of what this town had to offer.

While Erin waited for a reply, Samantha made a call to the repair shop. "Hey, Frank. I've got a car with a flat here out in front of the station. Do you think you could come by and plug it this afternoon?"

She listened while Frank ran through his tasks for the afternoon out loud, his brain processing at peak Frank Speed today. Then he came to the conclusion that he could take a look in a couple hours.

"Great. Thanks, Frank." She ended the call and returned her attention to Erin. "He'll fix it up in a little while. If you want to leave the keys with me, I can keep them at the station and make sure someone gets the car back to you this evening. I can have him call you when it's done, so you know when to expect it."

"That would be great, thanks." Erin's phone dinged, and she frowned at it.

"Problem with that ride home?"

"Yeah," she raised her eyes and shook her head. "I mean, no, not really. Zach's just tied up at work for a bit. Something about a Maltese and diarrhea I do not need the details on. He'll swing by for me in a little while though."

"Are you sure I can't drive you?" Something deep in Samantha screamed out for the answer to change, despite knowing that crushing on Erin was a very bad idea for so many reasons.

"You've helped already today with Addie." She looked down the short strip of Main Street behind them. "I can kill some time around here. I'll go poke the people at the bank, see if my transfer paperwork is ready to sign and finalize."

"You know where to find me if Zach can't make it." Samantha held out her hand. "Want me to take the key for Frank?"

Erin twisted the car key off the main ring and handed it to Samantha. Their fingers grazed each other in the exchange, and the sensation sent tingles all the way up Samantha's forearm.

Was she really so starved for touch that a mere key exchange got her all tingly?

Or was it this particular person's touch that set her off?

"Thanks," said Erin, snapping Samantha's attention

back to the woman's face and away from the soft skin of her fingers.

Those fingers that Samantha wanted to lace with her own and squeeze and hold tight and...

"No problem." Samantha held up the key and smiled, taking a step backward and landing right smack against the parking meter. She winced and tried to recover gracefully. Grace had never been her strong suit. "I'll have Frank call you when it's ready. Or I'll do it. Uh, call you. When it's ready. The car, I mean."

Smooth, Sam. Real smooth.

Erin smiled and returned the rest of her keys to her bag. Then she tucked one side of that delicious turquoise hair behind her ear and headed in the opposite direction toward the bank.

Samantha watched as she walked away. Not creepily. Although... maybe. She was failing at everything else today. Including standing, walking, and *existing*. Which was why she stood still and waited for Erin to cross the road before she turned to enter the station. She could only handle one mortifying stumble into a parking meter per encounter.

With Erin safely across the street and near the bank, Samantha headed into the police station to eat her sandwich, update Dustin on the morning's interviews, and *not* think about Erin Sonnier and her soft hands the rest of the day.

Chapter Twelve

"MCFLYYYYYYYY!"

Erin pulled her key from the door and held it open for Zach. Despite the events of the previous day, she'd been fine coming back here alone. Zach, however, wasn't as fine with the idea. He insisted he'd feel better walking inside with her and making sure everything was okay, since he was already there after driving her home.

"See, everything's fine."

"You thought everything was fine when you came up here yesterday, too."

"Okay. We'll make a sweep through the house," Erin said. "Will that make you feel better?"

"Much better."

His wide grin erased any annoyance that might have been creeping up. She'd forgotten what it felt like to have friends. Sure, she'd made new friends in New Orleans, but they weren't pick-you-up-when-you-had-a-flat friends. Certainly not rush-over-when-you-found-a-dead-body friends or sweep-the-house-for-new-dead-bodies friends.

They headed to the kitchen first, and after a quick peek inside the walk-in pantry, Zach followed her down the hall.

"It's just knowing you're alone here. Makes me nervous is all."

She held back from saying, *I'm used to being alone.* That sounded sad. And probably more dangerous. But the truth was, most of the time, she was just fine being alone.

"McFly! McFly! McFly!"

Erin jumped as they reached the bathroom doorway. "Chill Marty, jeez."

The poor bird had been used to Grandpa being home all day. He was probably going to freak out like this every time she left him alone for more than a couple of hours.

"I got it." Zach went ahead of her to peer inside the hall bathroom. "All clear."

"I'm pretty sure yesterday was a total fluke."

Or that one crime in this house per visit was all the universe planned on subjecting her to.

"Still gonna make a round in this place, anyway."

"Fine. Let's get on with it, if you insist."

She followed him down the hallway, pausing to look in the spare bedroom while Zach walked inside and opened the closet door, then peered under the bed. Her old bed. The one she was sleeping in while she was here, because it didn't feel right to seep anywhere else.

Her bright blue chevron comforter still sat on the

bed, along with the same yellow curtains and light gray walls from when she lived here. Her little desk and chair sat by the window with a view of a crepe myrtle tree.

"Next." Zach breezed past her and entered her grandfather's bedroom.

Erin remained in the hall for that one. She hadn't been able to cross that threshold yet. Going through that room was a Tomorrow Erin job.

"All clear," he said a minute later after checking the closet, bed, and master bathroom.

"Told you." She tried to sound sure of herself, but a wave of unexpected relief washed over her. She hadn't truly expected more trouble to pop up, but she still had some lingering anxiety after yesterday's surprise. "You know you can't do a house sweep every time I get home."

Home? This was not home.

So why did that word feel so good?

He frowned with disappointment, then brightened. "Want me to bring you a dog tomorrow?"

"Uh... no."

"A big one?" He wagged his brow. "Come on. A big, slobbery, barky one. Yeah, that would make me feel better!"

"That would *not* make *me* feel better." But she laughed anyway.

She'd been laughing a lot the last few days, considering the circumstances. Erin had expected to be downright miserable here, but being in this place and being around friends—both old and new—had been such an unexpected mood boost. She wished now even more that she could have dragged herself out here for the funeral. As much as that would have sucked, it might have helped her get through the initial grief sooner.

"McFlyyyyyyyy!"

The bird bobbed up and down and yanked his neck from side to side like he was doing some kind of grotesque dance.

"You sure? Marty would love a new furry friend to keep him company."

"Uhhhh, Marty isn't sticking around either," Erin said. No how. No way. She could *not* take a bird to her apartment. Not even if she wanted to. "And have you forgotten that I don't actually plan on living in this house?"

Zach scratched the back of his head. "Right. Kind of did forget that."

She bumped his arm. "You could always move to New Orleans. I'll probably need an extra roommate if I can't get out of here soon and lose my job and can't pay my rent." Her stomach turned just thinking about it. "Speaking of money. I need to get to work. I saw I had some online sales the last couple of days that I need to fill and take to the post office tomorrow."

"Gotcha." He awkwardly pointed his thumbs toward the door in a dorky move. Like the dork she'd forgotten she missed so much. "I'll get out of your way."

"Do you think you could drop me off at the post office before work tomorrow if they can't drop my car off before then?"

"No problem."

Her phone rang inside her bag on the couch and the screen flashed an unknown local number. "That's probably the mechanic. Sam said she'd give them my number to call when they were done."

When she answered the call, a man's gravelly voice greeted her with a mismatched cheerful tone.

"This is Frank, over at the repair shop. Is this Erin?"

"Yes. Is the car ready? Because I can—"

"No ma'am, I was just calling to tell you it won't be ready until at least early tomorrow afternoon. I have to find a tire to replace it, and I don't have one to match here."

"The nail was that big? You can't just plug it?"

"Ma'am, that wasn't a nail." There was silence on the other end. For a second, Erin thought she'd lost the connection, but the mechanic eventually spoke again. "You sure pissed someone off good."

The universe was definitely out to get her, but she got the sense that wasn't what this guy meant. "I don't understand. What was in it?"

"Nothing was in it," Frank said. "Someone slashed your tire."

"*What?*"

Zach took a step closer, his brow furrowed with concern at her shriek.

"I'll have a new one on there for you tomorrow. I'll give you a call as soon as I've got it ready to go."

Erin barely stuttered a thanks before the call ended.

"Problem?" Zach asked just as Marty squawked, mimicking the same pitch she'd used a moment ago.

"No, just a delay."

Erin couldn't tell him the truth. She couldn't form the words that someone hated her enough to slash her tire. She'd barely been in town for three days. Who'd she piss off so badly in that little time?

The memory of those accusations being flung at her a few hours ago flashed through Erin's mind.

No.

Addie would never go that far.

Would she?

"Car will be ready tomorrow afternoon," Erin said.

No sense giving Zach more reasons to worry about her. She had locks on her doors and a very loud feathered alarm.

"McFly! Marty. Marty."

She'd be fine.

Chapter Thirteen

SAMANTHA SIPPED HER WHITE WINE, but barely registered the lightly sweet taste of the Pinot Grigio someone had handed her a few moments ago.

What she really wanted to do was chug it and grab another. Maybe toss back a shot of bourbon. But that wouldn't be a good look for the woman running for chief of police at an animal rescue charity dinner.

Her sister had scheduled this appearance months ago. Long before either of them had any idea Samantha would be distracted by a murder case or that her ex-husband might be a suspect.

Nathan was there also. He was drinking whiskey on the rocks, laughing with the town's bank manager and a town councilman, and completely unbothered.

Samantha wasn't surprised to see him there. He attended most of these things. She was, however, surprised to see him elbow to elbow with a pretty blonde wearing dramatic fake eyelashes and a low-cut, floor-length green dress.

Rhea Blanchard.

Nathan's alibi and mistress.

No surprise seeing her there, either. Rhea was married to the bank manager, Lane Blanchard, who flanked her and was currently boasting about his whiskey collection to Nathan. Rhea appeared along with him at every society event and fundraiser in the parish.

She was also notoriously bored as heck with life in rural Louisiana.

But she would never publicly taint her reputation and risk her hold on her husband's money or status. Meaning there was no way she'd give Nathan an alibi on the record.

Rubbing elbows with her in public was a dangerous move. Her husband had a notorious temper on top of his notorious whiskey habit. If Lane caught wind of anything suspicious happening with his wife, Nathan might make news on the opposite end of a homicide.

"I see you're taking my investigation *very* seriously."

Samantha clenched her jaw and indulged her rage for five full seconds, imagining Jordan Fonseca ground up between her teeth.

As she released that tension in her jaw, Samantha raised her chin, relaxed her shoulders, and turned to her nemesis.

"Deputy Fonseca." She gave her best professional smile. The smile of a confident officer of the law. "I didn't think we'd get the pleasure of seeing you here today. What a delightful surprise."

Jordan was in a suit instead of his dark green uniform, and his hair had an extra layer of product, making it look shiny and downright crunchy. He held his own glass of brown liquid and looked like he was as comfortable in this room as he was at a crime scene.

He raised his glass and winked at her.

"Pleasure's all mine."

Even if he didn't behave like her ex-husband, and even if he wasn't her opponent, she would still hate this man with every cell in her body.

Samantha didn't go around hating people. Her job was to protect and serve. She couldn't do either of those well with hate festering inside her.

But she made an exception for two men in this town. Both of whom were in the same room with her at that very moment.

"So, Sergeant Ardoin, I'm assuming since you have time to make appearances, that means you've got a solid lead in our case?"

Our case.

Technically, he was right. She was running point, but her department was working cooperatively on this with the parish.

But Jordan only said that to crawl under her skin.

And she was letting him.

Get it together, Sam.

She needed to stay cool and deliver this speech in front of Etta's wealthiest and most powerful citizens. She needed them to fork over their cash for the parish humane society *and* fork over their votes for her next Saturday.

"I've got a couple leads," she said. "Need to follow up on new statements."

The weasel of a deputy standing before her tsk-tsked. "Shouldn't you be following up on those instead of rubbing elbows?"

It had only been two days since Paul's murder. Two days of investigation. The tox screen and autopsy weren't anywhere near her desk yet. She was doing her job. Jordan was just poking her. And she was letting him.

"Seeing as how some of the people I need to follow up with are in this room, I think I'm in exactly the right spot."

He raised an eyebrow at that and gave a low whistle. "Sure you're up for this, honey?"

Bait, Sam. Bait.

Don't bite.

"I'd be glad to take over for you," he added, his voice dripping with condescension. "I mean, the conflict of interest alone is... problematic."

In this town, every interaction was a conflict of interest. But she did her best to keep things fair and proper. Which was more than anyone could say about Jordan Fonseca.

Before she could respond, her other nightmare walked up behind her to place both hands on her shoulders. "Good to see law enforcement here. I feel so very safe now."

Nathan stepped around her into view, his front-page smile out in full force as he patted Jordan on the back.

Yup. He was definitely funding her opponent's campaign.

In fact, she'd bet money on the fact that he was the one who'd bought Jordan a ticket for this event.

They were conspiring to rattle her.

And she hated that it was working.

Samantha couldn't afford to be rattled. She needed to project calm and confidence when she addressed the room in a few minutes. She needed the citizens of this town to know she could handle one measly ex-husband. If she couldn't manage that, how would she handle being police chief?

"Deputy Fonseca, could I have a moment with my lovely ex-wife before she's called to speak in front of all these people, please?"

"Why, of course. I'll find you both later, and you can catch me up on those leads of yours, Sergeant." He winked at her again as he left.

Once he was out of earshot, Nathan spun and turned on her.

"Samantha, let's be real here." His tone switched from smarmy weasel to manipulative jerk. It had been so long since she'd been witness to or recipient of such a switch that it startled her.

"What do you want?"

"Don't you think you should hand this case over to the Sheriff's department where it should be?"

"It's my case. I'm handling it." She could smell his

119

self-preservation as strong as his expensive cologne. "And it's none of your business, frankly."

"I'm just... *concerned* for you, Sam. You can't seriously think you belong here." He gestured around the room. "Or that you can handle this case alone." He put a hand on her arm, and she could feel the touch through her suit jacket, which made her want to vomit on his shoes. "Don't you think this is all just too big for you?"

She looked around the room. The mayor stood in the corner, talking to a state senator. The secretary of state was also nearby, chatting with the owner of a regional bank and their house representative.

She definitely didn't belong here. Why did she think it was a good idea to pretend like she did?

Maybe Nathan was right.

He almost never was. But what if, just this time, Nathan *was* right? What if all of this really was too big for her?

"Sergeant Ardoin?"

She turned toward the unfamiliar voice. A woman with a tablet tucked in one arm aimed her other arm at the back of the stage.

Right. The stage.

Samantha had a job to do. Besides questioning her ex-husband and his side-piece.

"Yes. I'm ready." She tried to sound confident. Cool. Not at all flustered. But her breath was shallow and quickened along with her heart rate.

The stage was empty now, but she'd soon be standing in front of that microphone. Under those lights.

Promoting a good cause and inevitably fielding questions about a case she hadn't the slightest clue how to crack. Yet.

She'd find the killer eventually, but reporters never wanted "eventually" for an answer. Neither did the people of this town. They wanted immediate results. And they deserved answers.

Maybe she simply wasn't the person who could give them what they needed.

Maybe they deserved better than her.

"We're about to begin," the woman said. "Follow me this way, please."

Samantha hurried to follow, focusing on her breath and the shoulders of the woman in front of her while ignoring the surrounding crowd.

But she couldn't quiet the doubt in her head or the too-familiar voice behind her, the one she wished she never had to hear again.

"Good luck!"

Erin stood in front of the glass doors and peered inside. She couldn't believe it. Only four days after that fire, Addie had this place back up and running. And almost exactly four days from the moment she arrived in town, Erin was once again somewhere she probably shouldn't be.

This time, Samantha wasn't here to stop her.

After all her errands and after she'd settled up with

Frank at the repair shop, Erin had swung in at the police station to thank Samantha for hanging on to the key... and to file a vandalism complaint against Addie. But the secretary told her Samantha had left early for a charity event. Some election ass-kissing, Erin figured.

She'd seen the campaign signs around town, but she couldn't figure out why anyone, much less Samantha, would want to be police chief here. It wasn't exactly a prestigious gig.

But Samantha was a Keller and an Ardoin by marriage, even if it was an ended marriage. Erin always had the impression that Samantha wasn't anything like the rest of her family, but she could have misjudged her. She was usually pretty spot-on in her assessments of people, but maybe Erin was blinded by... something.

She decided to blame the tight pants if she turned out to be this far off the mark, and Samantha really was a Keller through and through.

Erin didn't make it two feet inside the front doors when Addie appeared out of thin air. Her fists were pressed against her hips, one fist holding a hot pink towel that matched her blouse. The turquoise apron was out-of-control bright, but Erin kind of loved it. She secretly loved every outrageous detail about this place, but she'd never admit it to Addie.

"You've got some nerve, you know that?"

"Me?" Erin couldn't believe Addie was calling *her* out when *she* was the one who had some explaining to do. And, if Erin had anything to say about it, a tire replacement to pay for. "I came in here for a sandwich. You're the one who's got nerve."

"Girl, what are you talking about? This is *my* restaurant."

"I know that. And that was *my* tire. But you already knew that, didn't you?"

"Tire? What tire?" Addie shifted from anger to confusion to mama-bear-concern in a matter of seconds. "You been out in that sun too long? Heat index was dang near a hundred and ten earlier. You had any water today?" She pointed at a counter stool and swiveled it toward Erin. "Sit. Theresa, get me a glass of water!"

"I don't need a water," Erin insisted, but she sat on the stool, anyway. "Just a BLT to-go and an apology."

And maybe a check for damages.

Addie frowned. "Your grandpa would kill me if I didn't make sure you were all right, so you're gonna sit here and drink this water, so he doesn't haunt my butt."

"No one's haunting you," said Erin. "That's just your conscience."

A redheaded woman with the same bright blue apron and a name tag that said "Theresa" placed a tall glass of ice water on the counter in front of Erin.

She didn't realize how thirsty she was until she saw the condensation already dripping down the cold glass, but she sure as heck wouldn't give Addie the satisfaction of drinking that.

Addie pointed at the glass. "My conscience is clear. How's yours?"

"My conscience is just fine these days." Erin resisted

the urge to wet her lips.

"What's this nonsense about a tire? You really got a problem or heat stroke?"

Erin was beginning to doubt her theory now. Addie seemed genuinely confused. And Erin had seen this woman in action enough to know that she was definitely not this good of an actress. Addie wore every emotion on her sleeve.

Still, it was all she had to go on. Someone destroyed Erin's tire. Addie was the only one with a reason. Or at least with a visible grudge.

"You accused me of arson, stormed out of a cafe—"

"I did not storm out of anywhere!"

"—and then when I went outside to my car a few minutes later, *someone* had slashed my tire."

Addie's lip quivered slightly as the woman was at a complete loss for words.

Dang it. Erin had been sure it had to be her.

"You think *I* did that?"

"No one else was around," Erin said. "Especially no one else who hated me as much as you do."

Addie looked genuinely hurt by that. So much that Erin almost felt guilty about the accusation.

"I don't *hate* you," Addie said, her voice wavering slightly.

"You sure act like it."

Her and everyone else around here. Erin was used to it. They all thought whatever they wanted about her, and they all decided long ago how Erin fit in their little pecking order. Spoiler: she didn't fit at all.

So she was used to people hating whoever they thought she was.

She just wasn't used to the vandalism.

Or the murder.

"I…" Addie paused, hunting down the right thing to say. "I just thought your grandpa gave you too much leeway. Since your parents… well, I know that was hard on everyone. Y'all were doing your best, but you have to know you didn't always make the greatest choices."

That was fair.

Dang it. She didn't come here to agree with Adeline Weaver about anything.

"Wait a minute." Addie slammed her towel on the counter and pointed a pink-painted finger at Erin. "You thought I stuck a knife in your tire, and you came here to call me out on it?" She lowered her hand onto the counter and looked Erin up and down. "You don't scare easy, do you?"

"Never have."

Addie nodded. "Good. Stay right there. And drink that."

She disappeared into the kitchen, leaving Erin alone at the counter.

Aw, hell.

She picked up the sweaty glass and took a long gulp of ice cold water, closing her eyes as the welcome liquid quenched her thirst and awakened her senses. She took gulp after gulp, glad Addie wasn't around to see she was right about Erin needing water, then placed the empty glass back on the counter.

The ice woke her brain up. Now that she was thinking clearly and could probably rule out Addie, she realized she had no idea who slashed her tire. Or why.

It couldn't be some random jerk. Could it?

She ran through everyone she'd come into contact with so far, and they all either couldn't have done it because they were somewhere else or didn't have a reason she could think of.

While she was mulling through a mental town census, Addie returned with a big bag containing more than one measly BLT.

"Since you've got a set of nerves on you, I've got a job for you." She placed the bag in front of Erin and handed her a sheet of order pad paper with an address on it.

"I don't need a job."

"No, but you're gonna do *this* job for me."

"Why?"

"Because there's a free BLT in there for you, too." Addie waved the paper at her again. "Take the rest of the order to this address."

Erin stared at the bag and paper in disbelief. "Don't you have someone else who can do this? I can pay for my sandwich."

"No, I need *you* to bring this." Addie glanced around and lowered her voice. "Didn't you see the news?"

"The news? No. Why?"

"Just take this. You'll see why when you get there." She placed the paper in front of Erin and took the empty glass without a word about it. "Please."

Chapter Fourteen

SAMANTHA REACHED for a beer in the fridge, not paying attention to which she grabbed from a mixed case of regional brews, a birthday gift from her brother-in-law earlier that summer. She popped the top and took a long swallow of whatever it was.

She nearly choked on it.

Super hoppy. Borderline skunky. And somehow sweet and fruity. Definitely not her favorite.

But it was easy to grab and kept her from shooting straight whiskey. Or drinking it directly from the bottle.

Dexter was still asleep in the bedroom. He could sleep through anything except a stranger's voice in the house. Just as well. She wasn't in the mood for company. Not even his. Not after the day she'd had.

Before she reached the couch, a knock on the front door echoed through the living room.

No one visited unannounced.

Her sister, maybe, but she'd already texted after

seeing the news. Plus, she was home with a sick kid. and her husband wasn't getting back from a work trip until tomorrow morning. No one else would just show up like this. Especially knowing what kind of mood she had to be in.

Unless it was Nathan here to gloat.

But even he wouldn't bother. He'd succeeded in his mission. He'd watched her fall on her face. His guy was sure to win the election now.

Nothing more he wanted from her.

Samantha opened the door without bothering to look. Didn't make a difference. She would tell whoever it was to go away.

But on the other side of the door, she found a bright head of blue-green hair and a shocked expression that matched her own.

"Uh, hi." Erin fidgeted with the ends of one side of her hair.

Samantha eyed her curiously. Erin didn't seem the type to show up on a porch looking to cheer up a practical stranger. She wasn't like the rest of the town that needed to bring over a sympathy casserole or pie for every occasion. *Here's a sorry-you-lost-the-election cobbler. Better luck next time.*

But Erin had run into her own troubles since she'd been back in town. Could that be why she was here? Samantha was so deep into her own pity party that she hadn't considered this might have nothing to do with her.

"Is something wrong?"

Erin held up the bag in her hand. "Addie sort of sent me here."

"Of course, she did." Samantha laughed, then took a sip of her beer. She hadn't planned on even a tiny chuckle this evening, but two seconds of Erin at her door and that's what she got. Well, thanks to Addie. "Come on in. You can have one of these and tell me how she convinced you to do her dirty work."

Erin stepped inside and looked around. "Sorry about the ambush. I didn't know this was your address."

"I figured." Samantha went to the kitchen and returned with an opened amber lager. "Here. I don't know if it's good, but it has to be better than the one I have."

"Thanks." Erin took the beer and tasted it. "It's nice."

Samantha was relieved she hadn't offered another nasty brew. Although she shouldn't be offering anything. She was supposed to be drinking and wallowing alone.

"So Addie roped you into coming here?"

"Apparently. I just went in to get a sandwich and maybe accuse her of slashing my tire."

"Wait... *what?*" Since when had Erin's tire nail turned into vandalism? And how had Addie landed on the suspect list?

Too many crimes for one tiny town lately.

Nathan and Jordan were both right. This was all too big for her.

"Not important. She didn't do it. Although, someone did, and I don't know who yet." Erin barely paused for a breath. "Anyway, she gave me my sandwich for free, but it came with an extra order and an address to deliver it to." She smiled awkwardly. "So, here I am. But I'm not sure why I'm here if you didn't order food."

Samantha opened the bag and pulled out both containers, handing the one with "BLT" written on it to Erin. "I guess you didn't watch the news."

"Why does everyone keep asking me that?"

Samantha was saved from having to answer and relive her horrifying performance by furious yapping.

Her black pug barged into the room and stood at Erin's feet, demanding to know who had entered his domain.

"Hey there." Erin looked down at the dog, clearly unsure whether to touch it or keep all her fingers intact.

Samantha scooped him up. "This is Dexter. Don't mind him. He's got to put up a front. He's a softie, really."

"Dexter. As in the serial killer and secret weapon of cops?"

"The one and only." Samantha kissed his little smushed face and set him back on the floor. As promised, he dropped his fierce act and plopped onto Erin's shoe.

"I like it." She grinned at Samantha. "And I like your sense of humor. It's subtle."

A sense of humor would have helped today. But no, she had to go all deer-in-the-headlights. Stumbling over her words. Letting the whole parish know she had no clue what she was doing with this murder case.

"Dexter and I were just about to drown our sorrows, but now that you're here, I suppose we can share the experience."

She finished her beer and went to the fridge to grab another.

"Um, and eat," Erin called out. "You should also definitely eat something."

Samantha returned and placed her beer on the little dinette table between the kitchen and living room. She opened the second container expecting to find a sandwich, maybe another BLT to match Erin's, but she found something else instead.

Samantha laughed.

Erin leaned across the table to peek inside the container. "Shrimp étouffée? I don't get it. Why is that funny?"

"It isn't." Not really. Samantha just found it funny that she hadn't expected it. "When I was ten, I was out riding my bike and fell in front of Addie's. Scraped the whole side of my leg pretty bad, but I wasn't supposed to be riding out that far, so I just sat in the ditch and cried. Addie carried me inside and didn't even ask if I wanted her to call my mother. She knew as well as I did I wasn't supposed to be there. She just helped me clean up and fed me a plate lunch and a Coke before dropping me off at home. The lunch that day was shrimp étouffée. I must have been hungry, because I cleaned off that plate."

"Addie's good people," Erin said reluctantly. "Don't tell her I said that."

Samantha nodded. "She's tough as a cane stalk, but she has her soft spots. And her love language is definitely food."

Erin dove into her sandwich while Samantha mixed

her rice and shrimp as the scent of the rich, garlicky sauce made her mouth water.

"So what happened with your tire?" she asked. "I thought it was just a nail?"

"Nope. Clearly intentional, according to Frank. But that's all I got," Erin said. "What's your story? Why did Addie send me here, and why does everyone keep asking me if I saw the news?"

Samantha wiped her mouth with a paper napkin. Stalling? Maybe. But what did she care? The whole town, except for Erin, already knew the truth. Erin would hear it eventually. Not that she had any reason to be concerned about what Erin thought, anyway.

Keep telling yourself that.

"Good news for the town: they'll get Jordan Fonseca as their Chief of Police."

Erin stared her down, trying to puzzle through what Samantha had just said. "I don't get why that's good news. Or how that happened. Did I miss the election? I thought it was next weekend?"

"It is. But it's a done deal now." She sighed and tossed her napkin on the table. "I blew it."

"Blew what? I tried to stop by the station to thank you for holding my key, but they said you were at some appearance or something."

"It was supposed to be a nothing event. Shake a few hands. Make a short speech for a good cause. Smile. Go home."

Dexter pawed at her leg, so Samantha picked him up.

He settled in on her lap, eying her half-eaten container of food.

"I'm guessing it didn't go exactly as planned. What happened?"

Samantha scratched Dexter's neck. "My ex happened. And Jordan Fonseca, who my ex is obviously financing in this race." She shook her head. "I let him get under my skin, and when reporters started asking me about Paul's case, I just... froze."

"What an asshat." Erin's face projected fury, but she reined it in and said, "I'm sorry. But I'm sure it wasn't as bad as you think."

"Oh, it was bad. Why do you think everyone's vaguely referring to the news?"

Erin grimaced. "But it's just one thing."

"That's all it takes."

"I don't believe that." Erin shook her head. "Of course, I don't believe one cop can save the whole system, but I can tell that you believe it. And you somehow make the people around here believe it, too. They'll all have your back on Election Day the same way you always have theirs every other day."

Samantha scoffed. "Nathan was right. They deserve better."

"Now *that* is a load of bullshit." Erin held up both of her hands. "Sorry, but I don't see what you ever saw in that slimy turd."

Samantha shrugged. It was the question she'd been asking herself over and over for years. "I was young.

Didn't know what I really wanted, and he had a plan for me so I didn't have to come up with one myself."

Erin's lips eased into a sad but sympathetic smile. "I get that." She tilted her head, like Dexter when he was trying to figure her out. "And now?"

Samantha was pretty certain she knew the real question behind that, but she wasn't as certain she was ready to give the real answer. Or at least the full one.

Yes, she was also attracted to women.

Yes, she was definitely attracted to the woman sitting in front of her right now.

"Now I'm not so young," Samantha said instead. "And now I know what I want."

Erin's smile stretched wider, her bottom lip jutting out just a little more.

Stop looking at her lips, Samantha kept reminding herself.

"Good answer," Erin said. "I just have one more question."

Samantha braced herself. "Okay, shoot."

"Why do you want to be police chief, anyway?" There was no derision in Erin's voice. No judgment. Only curiosity, like she was trying to solve the puzzle that was Samantha. "That job seems like an awful lot of political crap. Do you actually like that kind of stuff."

That Samantha could answer.

"Not at all. It is a lot of political crap, but that's part of why I want the job."

"Now I'm really confused," Erin said.

"I want to do what I can to separate the politics from

the police department. Unlike Jordan, I don't plan on playing any power games or dealing in favors."

If anyone knew how favors and family benefits worked, it was Samantha. She'd seen it through her own family, then witnessed the same things after she married into Nathan's family.

Erin was quiet for a long while, then she said, "Trey told me about how you helped him instead of charging him after his accident. I'm sure there are a whole bunch more stories like that of you doing the right thing. But Sam, you have to know you can't change it all by yourself. And not because you aren't good enough, but because it won't always be you who shows up when someone needs help. The system might be too messed up for you to fix alone."

"I know." Samantha hiccuped, the perfect excuse to swallow the sob that had been building. "I know I'm probably being naïve. But I have to try."

There was a long stretch of silence between them. Too long. Samantha was afraid that sob might escape after all.

"You, Samantha Keller Ardoin, are a much better person than I am," Erin said with a soft laugh. "When I want to burn down the patriarchy, I don't try to fix it. I light a match and take the whole town down with me."

Samantha grabbed her beer. "Once again, I *cannot* hear this."

They both smiled, though, and each took another sip.

"Okay, my turn for a question."

Jeez, she needed to slow down. The pitch of her voice

and the uptick in speed of the words tumbling out of her mouth were the equivalent of speaking in emojis.

"All right." Erin leaned back in her chair and wiped the crumbs—all that was left of her beloved BLT—from her hands. "Your turn. Shoot."

"Why'd you wait so long to come home?"

The whole vibe deflated with that question. Even Dexter grunted and hung his head over her thigh.

That was her. On brand. Buzz Kill Sam.

Instead of rightfully telling her to take a hike, Erin considered the question. Eventually, she found an answer she was satisfied with. "It hurt too much."

That wasn't the answer Samantha had expected. She didn't know what exactly she'd expected, but it wasn't that.

"I meant to, to visit Grandpa from time to time, but I couldn't bring myself to come back to a town that had never wanted me in the first place."

"But you had him. Your grandfather," Samantha said. "And Zach."

And me.

But they'd been barely acquaintances, much less friends, so she didn't add herself to the list. Admittedly, it was a short list.

"I called him. A lot. Well, a lot for me. And I wanted to see him, but I just didn't." She took a big breath and exhaled, long and slow. "Then it was too late." She averted her eyes and blinked a few times. "I know everyone probably thinks I was just being selfish or whatever in not coming to the funeral, but I was in bed for a full week. Crying. Taking pills. Trying to figure out why the universe hates me so much. Why it would take everything from me, and then find a way to take even more."

Blinking could no longer stop the tears, and Samantha watched helplessly while Erin wiped them away.

She wasn't exaggerating. The universe really had taken so much from her. First as a little girl when she'd lost her parents.

It had been such a freak accident. Samantha remembered hearing the explosion. The counselors who'd been brought in for students struggling to process the accident. The funerals. The endless string of reports that made the national news.

It had been a plane crash, only Erin's parents weren't in the plane. They'd been in the parking lot of a local bakery, picking up Erin's birthday cake. Erin was at school, but she'd heard the crash along with everyone else.

Samantha remembered hearing that tiny plane fly over before it lost control, tried to land in a nearby field, then crashed straight into her parents' car. The plane broke into several pieces, and the explosion ignited the smashed car with her parents in it. Everyone on board the plane died as well as Erin's parents, and a few bystanders were hospitalized with injuries and burns. It was a fluke. An accident that no one could have predicted. A monumental event of wrong place at the wrong time.

From that moment on, Erin lived with her grandfather. He did his best and loved her as much as he could in her parents' place. As far as Samantha could tell, he'd done an amazing job. Especially considering how that accident must have traumatized Erin.

The town, however, didn't have a clue what to do with Erin.

Some, like Addie, went hard on her, feeling that Erin needed the firm guiding voice her parents could no longer provide.

Some doted on her, giving her whatever she wanted. Denying her nothing. This mostly came in the form of casual friends, people with spare pills, weed, or beer. Sometimes it came from girlfriends who gave and gave while Erin took until they had nothing left to give.

But most in town just ignored her. Stayed out of her way. Pretended she didn't exist. Like whatever curse she had might be catching. Samantha always figured those responses had to sting the most. Or at least do the most damage.

And now she'd lost the one person who'd done right by her. Samantha's heart could hardly bear it. How Erin was here, living and breathing through all of that loss, was a testament to the woman's strength and resilience. Samantha wished she had a mere fraction of that.

"I'm sorry. I should go." Erin stood abruptly and pushed her chair in. "I didn't mean to barge in on your pity party with my own."

"There's plenty of room in this party for two." She smiled sympathetically, but Erin headed backward toward the door, anyway. "Besides, you brought food, and I invited you in. That's not barging. And you've got way more things to worry about than me and my failed campaign."

Erin reached the door and held it open. She stood there for a second, then turned to face Samantha, who was now just inches away.

Samantha's head was swirling as she gripped the side of the door for support.

"It's a little more than that, and we both know it." Erin looked deep into her eyes. "And it's more than just caring about this town. That jerk messed with your head. You have a right to be upset. And it wasn't the first time, I'm guessing?"

Samantha nodded, struggling to push down the lump forming in her throat. Struggling even more not to think of all the times he made her feel small. Weak. Incapable of being anything but less than.

Erin reached a hand up and placed it against the side of Samantha's face. Her palm was cool—still cool from holding that bottle—against Samantha's cheek. She held Samantha's gaze with those bright blue eyes.

"You deserve so much better than that." She inched closer, eliminating the space between them. "He never for one second deserved you."

As the last word fell from her lips, Erin's mouth brushed against Samantha's. Fuzzy-headed and too tired to deny herself or think about what the responsible thing in this situation would be, Samantha leaned forward to press her mouth to Erin's. She felt Erin smile against her, as pleased with this turn of events as Samantha. Her hand slid from Samantha's cheek to wrap around behind her head, holding her close.

Samantha couldn't remember the last time she'd kissed anyone. The last time she'd *wanted* to kiss someone this badly. The last time she'd felt wanted in return.

Every cell in her body radiated with heat. She wanted more. So much more. She wanted to pull Erin back inside the house and forget all about the rest of the day.

But Erin removed her mouth, then slid her fingers down a strand of Samantha's hair. The gentle tug sent tingles through Samantha's scalp and down her spine.

"I should go." Erin's voice was a husky whisper, her mouth still just inches away. Well within reach again.

Samantha tried not to take the statement as a rejection. She'd probably be the one to shut things down herself if she'd been completely sober.

But she wasn't. And she didn't want Erin to go.

She grazed her fingers down Erin's arm until she reached her hand and squeezed it. "You don't have to."

Erin inhaled and rolled her eyes, a playful smile of frustration still on her face. "I don't know what this town is doing to me. Or maybe it's you rubbing off on me. But you're not exactly in a state of mind for making clear decisions, so I'm going to make what I hope is a good, responsible choice and leave. Now. Before I change my mind."

Samantha pouted in protest.

Pouted.

Jeez, she'd downed that beer quicker than she'd intended. Well, no, she'd drunk it exactly as fast as she'd intended. She'd just never intended for Erin to show up.

Erin gave another too-quick kiss, then took a step backward on the porch. "I'll see you later."

Samantha waved awkwardly, not sure what to do with her hands anymore. "Thanks for the food!"

Erin waved back. As she reached the car, she shouted, "Thank Addie! She's become quite the town matchmaker."

"Town meddler is more like it!"

"I'll take it either way." Erin closed the car door and gave one last wave through the window before driving off.

The sun hadn't fully set yet. That late summer sunset with the orangey-pink haze blanketed the surrounding fields.

Samantha went back inside where Dexter stood in front of the door, staring up at her. Silently judging her. But it seemed she had his approval because he grunted and wobbled off to bed now that their guest had exited and the excitement was over for the evening.

That left Samantha completely alone. Something she was used to. Something she should be fine with.

She looked over at the empty containers and bottles on the table.

Two sets.

She didn't know what any of this meant. Her desire for company. Her complete failure today. Inevitably losing the election. Her feelings for Erin. That *kiss*.

She wasn't someone who did things like that. Something so impulsive. Something that felt so good.

For the first time ever, she decided not to worry about anything. She planned to watch TV with Dexter and not think about any of it. Those were Tomorrow Samantha's problems.

Chapter Fifteen

ERIN SLIPPED the last bead on the head pin. Then she grabbed her pliers to form a loop and attached a jump ring to connect the ear wire.

She lifted the completed pair, checking that the beads on each lined up correctly and that the loops were the same size and shape, and that nothing looked wonky. She shifted them in the light, examining her craftsmanship from different angles.

Perfect.

Her shoulders relaxed with a tiny sigh of satisfaction. Making jewelry always provided a sense of focused calm. Better than any meditation app.

She slipped them onto a card and into her "done" box.

Only forty-nine more pairs to go.

The sort-of-good news was that a tropical storm had popped up in the gulf and took aim at New Orleans. Forecasters weren't expecting major damage or evacuations, but the store would be closed for a day or two, giving Erin a few extra days to settle things here in Etta.

More good news was they'd sold out of her pieces at all the owner's locations and wanted a re-order delivered when she returned. Plus, she'd gotten more online orders than she'd planned for, so she needed to restock, package, and ship those, too.

Aside from money in her account, more orders meant more to do while she waited to finalize everything and sell this house... if this murder case ever got solved. More to do meant less time to think about a certain officer of the law and a certain kiss they'd shared.

She hadn't meant to kiss Samantha Ardoin. It just sort of happened.

No, that was a lie. Erin had *made* it happen. With an assist from Addie, of course.

She'd always wondered about Samantha, even though she'd only dated guys in school. Erin never suspected that was an act or a cover. But she'd also seen... something else. Something in the way Samantha had looked at her. Even back in high school, when Erin had been dating Sam's friend.

The more she thought, the more she remembered those little moments. Lingering glances. Tiny smiles. Last night's kiss proved it hadn't all been in her imagination.

But that didn't mean kissing Samantha had been a good idea. Far from it.

A knock on the front door set Marty squawking. Great. Her head was already pounding.

Erin pushed up, stretching her legs a bit before she hobbled over to see who it was.

"Just checking on my two favorite neighbors," Zach chirped as she let him in.

"We're practically your only neighbors. And barely that. There's a whole cane field between us."

"Details." He walked in and said hello to Marty, who began excitedly screaming his own name as usual.

"Have we discussed your future in bird ownership?" she asked.

"Not happening." He whistled at the spread on the living room floor. "Who threw up a craft store in here?"

"Good news, finally. That storm is buying me a couple days to fill these orders *and* finish up my business here."

"Lucky New Orleans."

She groaned, feeling a little guilty about her glee. The storm shouldn't be bad, but everyone in that area got twitchy whenever something even mildly big came near, and half the neighborhoods flooded in an afternoon shower thanks to the craptastic drainage. "But I definitely have to get back as soon as it passes. And bring this giant order with me."

Thankfully, she'd brought plenty of supplies with her. At least, she hoped she'd brought enough of everything. If she was short even a single pin or bead, there wasn't a nearby store to restock at and certainly not enough time to have anything shipped.

Zach held up a card holding dangling silver earrings with green and blue glass beads. "Pretty."

"Thanks. Those are my favorite."

He smiled and held them up to her hair. "Can see why."

"No, I just like those." She tugged at a strand near her face. "The hair changes. Sometimes monthly. If I stay much longer, you'll start seeing my roots."

"Like I don't remember your roots."

Erin happened to be knee-deep in her roots this week. Just so happened she was the only one who'd forgotten them.

"Soooooo." Zach sat on the floor cross-legged beside her, just like when they were kids playing board games in this very living room. "Heard you went to Addie's last night."

"Uh-huh."

She'd bet money he heard a lot more than that. And she'd double down on that being the real reason he'd come over. But she wasn't about to spoon-feed his own question to him.

"Did you really go down there and accuse Addie of slashing your tire?" His gleeful expression turned serious. "And when exactly were you gonna tell me someone slashed your tire?"

She shrugged. He'd get to his real question, eventually. No need to rush him.

She wasn't itching to talk to someone about what she did after she left Addie's. Nope. Not at all.

"You found out before I could tell you. And I'm pretty sure now that Addie didn't do it."

She put the earrings back in their box and started

packing up the rest of her supplies. She needed to take a break, and she had checks to write before the mail passed.

"But you thought she did and stormed down there, anyway?" Zach laughed. "I guess you haven't changed all *that* much."

"Guess not."

"So who did slash your tire? Any idea?"

"I was hoping you might help me figure out who besides Addie hates me that much."

"No idea." He shook his head. "You haven't even been here long enough to piss anyone else off yet."

"Gee, thanks."

"You're welcome. But between that and... you know. The other thing." He scratched at his head. "It's just creepy. That kind of stuff doesn't happen around here. You know that."

"Not like I had anything to do with it."

"I know, but..." He placed his hand on her arm to stop her from closing containers. "I'm just worried about you being here alone. I don't know why any of this is happening, but even if it's all just a big string of coincidences... I don't know. Maybe you should stay at my place? Or something. Maybe find someone to stay here with you?" He grinned and raised his brow. "Captain Tight Pants?"

Erin sighed and finished closing the containers and stacked them all beside the couch.

"I was wondering when you'd get to that. Of course, everyone knows I went there last night. Nothing slips by without notice in this town."

"You think Addie wasn't gonna gloat about her little plan?" His grin faded. "She was real worried about Sam. Lot of people were. How was she?"

"Upset," Erin said. "At first."

"And then?"

Erin gave a little grin of her own. "And then she wasn't."

He rubbed his hands together with glee. "Details. Gimme details."

She hit him with a couch pillow on the side of the head. "You're still the worst, you know that?"

"I do know that. Now tell me what happened. I mean, not the detail-details. Just... you know... more!"

"Not much, honestly. I met Dexter. We ate what Addie sent. Had a beer. She had two. We talked a bit. Then I left."

He eyed her appraisingly. "What did you skip?"

"Fine. I kissed her before I left. You happy?"

"Ec-freaking-static."

And he was. It was one of the things she'd always loved about being friends with Zach. He was genuinely happy for her whenever the rare gift from the universe came her way. No possessiveness. No jealousy. No angsty-dude-pining-for-the-town's-lesbian bullshit. It was an honest-to-goodness friendship. And she didn't have a good answer why she'd let it slip away all these years.

"So, what's the chance you get her to come here? Or you stay with her instead of being here by yourself? To ease my worries, since I know you don't give a rat's butt about your own safety."

"Zero. I'm lucky I got a kiss out of that. And it was all the beer anyway, I'm sure. No way she's moving that fast," Erin said. "Besides, it's fine."

"Erin, it's not fine."

"Listen, I know the universe has it out for me. But it's not chasing me out of this house. I finally dragged myself back here, so it's gonna take a lot more than a dead guy and a flat tire to send me packing before I'm ready."

And she wouldn't be ready for a few more days. Not until the storm passed and she at least finished the account transfers and settled bills for the next couple of weeks. Then she could go back to work for a while, and hopefully by the time she returned, she could put this house on the market.

"Still stubborn as ever."

"You know it." Erin reached over to the side table and grabbed the stack of bills and checkbook she'd put there earlier. She wrote out a check to the utilities company and set the cable bill aside to call and cancel tomorrow. Then, she licked the envelope shut. "Do you know where he kept the stamps?"

Zach narrowed his eyes and thought for a moment. "Not sure. Want me to check the junk drawer in the kitchen?"

"Yeah, thanks." But she had a sinking suspicion it wasn't in there. "Doubt you'll find it there, though. Grandpa was pretty old school."

"I mean, keeping stamps in a junk drawer is kinda

old school," he called out from the kitchen over the rumbling of who-knows-what in the drawer. "And new school. Isn't that where everyone keeps their stamps?"

She had no idea where most people kept anything. Her own organizational systems for everything except her jewelry-making supplies was... well, not exactly organized. Her roommate kept track of most of the bills and made a list of what Erin owed each month. Then Erin wrote a check for it all made out to her roommate. It was the easiest method for everyone involved.

So she had no idea where the stamps were in her own apartment, much less where her grandpa kept them. But she did remember his rather peculiar system for stashing important things.

Erin walked down the hall to her grandfather's bedroom and stood in the doorway.

Okay, Erin. You can do this.

"Not in here," Zach hollered from across the house. "Did he have a desk or something?"

"I'm back here!" she called out, still standing in the doorway.

When Zach walked up behind her a few seconds later, he put his chin on her shoulder. "Want me to look around for you?"

She shook her head. "I think I know where they are."

"I don't see a desk. Nightstand?"

"No." She took a deep breath and stepped into the room, heading for the far wall by the window where he kept a little reading nook in the corner. "Bookshelf."

Zach followed behind until they both stood facing

two tall bookshelves crammed with books. "He kept stamps in here?"

"He kept *everything* in here."

She scanned the shelves. All the books were alpha-betized by author for fiction and title for nonfiction. And yes, they were mixed on the shelves.

Stamps.

On the bottom half of the second set of shelves, she found the S's. Erin grabbed the worn paperback copy of *Doctor De Soto* and pointed at the spine. "Steig. For stamps."

When she opened it, they found the middle pages carved out where sheets upon sheets of forever stamps were stuffed inside the thin book.

"Holy crap," Zach whispered. "Did he think we'd still need postage post-apocalypse?"

"I don't know what that man thought," she admit-ted. "But he always did this. It was back here in his room, so I didn't see him get stuff often. I sort of forgot until just now."

Zach stared at the books in amazement. "What the hell else is in these?"

"I have no idea."

Cash, for sure. Under C. She was pretty sure which book. But what else?

A deep pit opened up in her stomach.

"Zach, what if Paul was looking for something? Something in one of these books?"

They both stared at the wall of books.

"Maybe," he said. "Sounds like as good a theory as

any. Especially since we don't have any other theories yet."

She felt nauseous as the pit widened and a sour taste filled her mouth. "What if someone killed him for something in one of these books?"

"Sounds crazy, but so does keeping five thousand stamps in a cut-out book." He turned his head to look at her. "Want a hand going through them, or you want to do this alone?"

Her eyes remained fixed on the books. "I could definitely use a hand with this."

Chapter Sixteen

SAMANTHA STABBED AT HER SALAD, ignoring the four pairs of eyes homed in on her. All waiting for her answer. All Keller eyes.

All except for her brother-in-law. But even he'd spent so much time with their family over the last ten years that he'd morphed into a Keller through osmosis.

"Well?"

Samantha set her fork down and looked at her mother at the head of the table. "I don't have a plan yet. And frankly, I don't know if I want one."

Her mother threw her hands up in exasperation. In the next chair over, her brother snort-chuckled, while her sister took a long sip of wine across from Samantha, and her brother-in-law tried to remain invisible. Par for the course for a family dinner.

"Can you believe this? Melanie, talk some sense into your sister, please."

Melanie set down her wine. "Okay, here's what we do next." Then she rattled off a list of plans like a drill sergeant.

Samantha had hoped at least Melanie would have her back. She'd always considered her sister to be her closest ally in the family. But Melanie was still a Keller, even if she had taken a back seat as a doting, supportive wife and mother happily ditching any aspirations of her own. Now she was taking this opportunity to live vicariously through Samantha's potential political career. Or maybe kick start her own second act as a campaign manager.

When Melanie finished detailing her battle plans, Samantha calmly said, "I don't know if I want to do that."

"What part?" Melanie asked.

"Any of it? All of it."

She watched as her mother's jaw fell slack.

Samantha had left out Nathan's part in the previous day's debacle. His interference and words would only add fuel to their fire. *Well, of course you have to prove him wrong*, they'd tell her.

She'd spent so much of her life proving people wrong. She was tired of it.

Maybe she didn't have to try so hard. Maybe people could believe in her or not. Maybe it was up to them and not her.

Why should she have to work doubly hard to prove yet one more thing to her ex-husband, who never once tried to prove that he was worthy of anything? To her or to anyone else.

Melanie drank more wine while the men excused themselves. They didn't even bother to come up with an excuse. Just got up and ran off like cowards. As if Samantha or Melanie would ever have been allowed to get away with that.

Silence stretched out long after they disappeared. Her mother stared her down from across the table.

Melanie downed the rest of her wine. "Shall I get us all a refill?"

"Sit."

When their mother commanded, they did as ordered. So Melanie sat.

Samantha, however, was not feeling quite so compliant.

"There isn't anything to discuss. I'm not dropping out of the race, but there will be no scrambling. No more appearances. No more anything but showing up to work and doing my job. The people here know who I am. What I stand for. What I'm capable of. If anyone needs to prove themselves, Jordan does."

"Yes, but you know that's not how any of this works."

"That's how it *should* work, and that's how I'm going to run the rest of my campaign. I'm going to focus on my investigation and protecting the people of this town, and that's all I have left to say about that."

Although Erin's voice was still running on a loop through her fuzzy memory of the previous night.

You can't change it all by yourself.

Maybe not. But Samantha had to try.

And she still had a job to do.

She sure as heck couldn't do any of that if she was spending all her time shaking greased palms and making pointless speeches.

It was her mother's turn to sip her cabernet, while Melanie shifted in her seat.

"How's the case coming, anyway?" Melanie's voice was soft and hesitant. Melanie was always the sweetest sibling, but hesitant was normally not her style. "Did you just panic up there, or do you really not have any leads?"

Her mother set down her glass and waited for the answer as well.

"I'm following up on a few things." Samantha cleared her throat. "You know I can't comment on an open investigation."

"I can't believe you haven't arrested that Sonnier girl yet," her mother said. "She rolls back into town with *her* criminal past, and there just happens to be a body in her house? We all know that girl is trouble. I don't understand why it's taking so long to arrest her."

Samantha stared at her mother. "We aren't arresting her because she didn't commit any crimes."

Her mother snorted. An uncharacteristic sound coming from her. Samantha had a knack for being the one person who could fluster Barbara Keller with her mere existence.

"Innocent until proven guilty, Mom," Melanie said,

proving she actually did have Samantha's back after all. Better late than never.

"You know as well as I do she burned down that shed," their mother said with contempt dripping from every word. "Conviction or not, everyone here knows it."

Her mother wasn't entirely wrong. Everyone knew that Erin had burned down Timmy Girard's parents' shed one hot August night much like this one. He'd gone around town telling everyone that he'd had his way with her in that shed. He said she'd come sneaking up to his house one night that summer, begging him to be her first, and he told everyone that he'd granted her wish.

The *real* rumor Samantha's mother hadn't heard or didn't want to believe was that when he'd asked her out, she'd told him she liked him well enough, but not like that. She'd confessed to him she was only into girls.

After a week of him spreading that story around school at the beginning of his and Erin's sophomore year, someone stole his LSU hat from his locker, nailed it to the front of that shed, and set the whole thing on fire.

Samantha never heard another rumor about Erin from that day on, and Chief Vidrine never found any evidence to file charges. All the town knew for sure was that Erin came into school the day after the fire with a spring in her step and her head held high.

Come to think of it, that might have been the exact day that Samantha fell for her. Pouring the foundation for her feelings. And the previous night's kiss had been that cement firming up for good.

Cement or not, she was too tired to defend Erin to her mother, especially knowing she'd never convince her, anyway.

Besides, a different route was called for here. Distraction. And a hell of a lead she hadn't explored yet.

"Actually, I still need to talk to Randy."

Her cousin's name instantly turned her mother's ears red as she glared across the table.

"Samantha Renee."

That tone. Samantha was more than familiar with it and what it meant, but she didn't care. Not tonight. Not anymore.

She was no longer interested in playing the role of dutiful Keller daughter. She'd *never* been interested in playing that role, but now she didn't care if her mother knew the full extent of her disinterest. It was past time, Samantha decided, that she got to play the starring role in her own life.

"I have to follow every lead. And he *was* working the day of Addie's fire. With those incidents back to back, we have to make sure there isn't a connection." She picked up her own wineglass. "Especially with *his* criminal past and all. He was at the restaurant the day of the fire, and he knew Paul. Weren't you suggesting I arrest Erin based solely on reputation and opportunity?"

She waited for her mother's own words to sink in.

It felt good having the upper hand for once. Even if only for a brief moment.

"That's different," her mother argued calmly.

"Why? Because he has our last name?"

"Frankly, yes."

Samantha hadn't expected her to be this honest about her nepotism.

"My job is to investigate a crime. Not look the other way when someone shares my last name."

Either of her last names.

Samantha straightened her back, and Melanie gave her a curious look.

She couldn't right now, but Samantha would explain to Melanie about Nathan backing Jordan. Later, when it was just the two of them, or over the phone when their mother wasn't around. Only because it indirectly concerned her campaign.

But after a crappy night's sleep, she was beginning to wonder if there was more at stake here than bragging rights to this election.

She'd been looking into Nathan because of his family's history with Paul, but what if he had an additional motive? After all, he thought this investigation was too big for her. He'd said so himself. What if he'd had a part in creating the crime in the first place? That would get Paul *and* Samantha out of his way and Jordan Fonseca in charge of the police force and in his pocket.

It sounded outrageous, even to her. But she couldn't ignore the possibility any more than she could ignore her delinquent cousin as a potential suspect.

Her phone buzzed on silent, and she felt a little rush seeing Erin's name flashing on the screen.

She pushed back her chair and stood.

"Where do you think you're going?" Her mother

continued to stare her down, struggling to maintain her calm and her illusion of control. "We haven't finished this discussion."

Samantha drained the last of her wine and waved her phone in the air. "Excuse me, I need to take this outside."

Chapter Seventeen

ONCE SHE SHUT the French doors behind her and stood on the elaborate brick patio in her mother's backyard, Samantha answered the call. Before she could say hello and relish the sound of that voice greeting her, she was met with a shrill, fast-paced string of phrases that made absolutely no sense.

"I don't understand," she said. "Slow down and tell me again."

"We were looking for stamps," Erin repeated, pausing to catch her breath. "And I just found a ton of prescriptions."

Samantha had no idea why Erin was calling right now to tell her that her aging grandfather had a bunch of medicine. Or why panic shredded the edges of Erin's voice.

"You were looking for stamps in the bathroom?" Samantha remembered the gentleman being a tad eccentric, but that sounded like an odd place to stash stamps, even for him. "I'm sure he was on a lot of medicines. Older body, more pills. That fun game."

"No, in his bedroom, and not actual medicine," Erin said firmly. "Written prescriptions. On paper. *Tons* of them."

"For what?" Samantha heard whispering in the background but figured it must be Zach. "I don't understand why you're so upset that he didn't fill his prescriptions."

Although she tried not to let on, Samantha grew more concerned by the second, thinking about a certain ex-husband's pharmacy and the doctors they worked with. Everyone knew there was truth to the vague rumors of shady business goings on, but no one was ever willing to come forward with any proof.

What if Erin had stumbled on proof?

"Is this why Paul was in the house?" Erin asked. "Could he have been looking for these?"

A chill ran up Samantha's back despite the hot August evening and lack of any breeze.

Samantha had already downed more wine than she should drive on, but this could be something big. Something that couldn't wait until tomorrow morning.

Crap. Tomorrow morning.

"Erin, can you put those back where you found them? I'm going to send someone out there to collect the prescriptions and bring them to the station." Dustin was on call. She'd have him take photos and bag them and put them on her desk. If that's what Paul had been after, it seems he never found them. Which meant they wouldn't find usable fingerprints or any other useful evidence on the papers themselves. But the prescriptions were still evidence. Maybe not in Paul's murder, but in taking down a few other criminals they'd had their sights on for years.

"You aren't coming yourself?"

Did she imagine the disappointment in Erin's question?

"I can't. I'm dealing with another thing. I'll be in touch tomorrow, though." Tomorrow. Crap, crap, crap. "But Erin, I need you to do something."

"I'll put them back in the book where I found them."

"In the book?"

"Yeah, in a hardcover copy of Terry Pratchett's *The Colour of Magic*. Pratchett. 'Pr' for 'prescriptions.'"

Samantha wasn't following that at all. Too much for one night.

"Yes, put them back until someone gets there. Thank you." She closed her eyes and refocused. "I need you to stay home tomorrow."

Erin went silent on the other end. Samantha took that as a very bad sign.

Eventually, Erin asked, "Why?"

How could Samantha say this without giving away too much? Without putting more ideas in Erin's head.

She admired Erin's ability to get things done—with or without matches—but Samantha needed her out of this investigation. For Erin's safety and to keep the whole thing uncomplicated. Or, at least, less complicated. She wasn't sure what was going on yet, but she had a feeling Erin was tangled in the middle of it. She needed to untangle her and figure this out.

"I need you to stay away from Paul's funeral."

The funeral had been scheduled for Tuesday, but with the storm picking up speed and leaning their way now, they'd pushed it up to tomorrow morning.

More silence. That definitely wasn't good.

"Erin?"

"I heard you."

"So you'll stay away, right? I just need to handle this myself, and I don't need to run interference with you jumping the gun on whatever you think you've figured out."

"I said, I heard you."

Samantha noted that Erin's response was not an answer to her very direct question.

She also knew she had no right to demand anything of Erin, and she'd probably already pissed her off with that last statement.

"I'm sorry. I didn't mean to order you around or anything, I just—"

"You think I'm going to mess everything up."

"I didn't say that."

"You don't have to. You think it. Everyone always thinks it. I'm the town screw-up, right? Always have been. Always will be."

"Erin, I'm sorry. I don't—"

"It's okay. I'll put these back and wait for the other

officer. Thank you for your help, Sergeant Ardoin."

"Erin—"

The line went silent. Samantha pulled the phone away from her ear to look at the screen.

Call ended.

She wasn't sure if she was more upset because she'd clearly hurt Erin or because she was fairly certain Erin was going to do the exact thing she'd asked her not to do.

Melanie peeked her head through the French doors. "All done with your call?"

Samantha realized she was still staring at her phone and let her arm drop. "Yeah, all done. Work thing."

"Uh-huh." Melanie stood beside her on the patio. They both stared off at the sun halfway below the horizon, leaving a warm pinkish glow over the western sky. "Your cheeks are redder than a white wine flush, and you never get this worked up over work. Ms. Calm, Cool, and Collected. Want to talk about it?"

More than anything, she wanted to tell Melanie everything. About Erin. About the kiss. About all the things she'd hidden from her sister over the years.

But she couldn't. Not because Melanie wouldn't keep her secrets, but because she didn't want to put Melanie in that position. She knew how hard it was to keep anything quiet in this town. Plus, there were already enough wedges in her family. She didn't want to be the cause of yet another battle line drawn between them all.

And she certainly didn't want to find out which side people would choose.

"Not really," Samantha said. "It'll all blow over by tomorrow. Always does."

"Going to the funeral?"

"Yeah. You?"

"I guess. Elliot is going, so I'll probably go with him and leave the kids with Mom. I'm sure she'll be glad for the excuse to stay home."

"But she'll miss the opportunity to wear her new funeral outfit."

Melanie folded her arms and leaned against the side of the house. "I mean, we could give her a reason to wear it. Bury her in it?"

"Why must I be surrounded by people who insist on broadcasting their criminal intentions?"

With a laugh, Melanie said, "You know I'm just playing." Then, with a lightning switch to serious, she said, "You know she'd haunt our butts if we didn't bury her in that blue ballgown she loves. The one she bought on the trip to *Paris*."

"One hundred percent. But she'll haunt me, regardless."

"Oh good, then you take the fall."

"Not on your life. I take the fall for everything else around here."

"That's just because you're amazing when you're being you, and she wants you to be her. Take that as the good thing it is."

Melanie meant well, but Samantha couldn't help feeling sickened by the comment. Sure, being a cop wasn't on her mom's agenda for Samantha's life, and her divorce was definitely not part of the plan either. But how much was Samantha really being herself? In all the other ways that mattered?

"I'm just tired is all," she said.

"Then stop caring about what she thinks."

"I can't care much less."

"Then let it go." Melanie looked behind them and leaned in to whisper, "Bail on the next one of these obnoxious dinner things."

"She'll just lay into you in my absence."

"I'm a big girl, Sam. I can take care of myself." She put her hands on her hips. "I don't know if you've noticed, but I am a grown-ass adult now."

"I know you are. I just don't want to leave you alone in the line of fire."

"Pfft." Melanie waved a hand. "I'll throw Chad under the bus. He's gotten off way too easy all these years."

"Truth."

"Besides," Melanie said, leaning her head against Samantha's shoulder. "I want my big sister happy."

Samantha wished she could say something about how she was already happy, but she couldn't lie right now. She felt very much on the verge of happiness, maybe for the first time in her life. But she wasn't there yet. She wasn't even sure if she could ever get there. Not in this town.

"I love you too, Melanie." She put her own head against Melanie's and breathed in the scent of her shampoo. It was light, clean, and very Melanie.

Her sister stood up straight and looked Samantha in

167

the eye. "Now, are you gonna let me help you win this election or what?"

"Honestly?" Samantha took a deep breath and said what had been running through her mind since last night. "I don't even know if I care about winning anymore. I mean, I do. For all the same reasons we discussed when I first decided to run." She was finding more reasons this town needed cleaning up with every second she was in this race, but Samantha shook her head. "I won't play dirty or play into anyone's pocket."

"Not even if the ends justify the means, and you could clean all that up in the future?"

"No," Samantha insisted. "I couldn't live with myself. And I've already lost too many sleepless nights in my life."

"Agreed," said Melanie. "I'm still team whatever-it-takes, but I respect your decision. So what *are* you gonna do?"

"Just what I said. I'm going to solve the case, even if it leads me to take down an Ardoin *or* a Keller."

"Wait... what?" Melanie leaned back and looked sideways at Samantha. "That must have been one helluva phone call."

"Maybe."

Melanie smirked. "I thought it was just some secret thing you've got going on."

"What makes you think I have some kind of secret thing?"

"Oh, please," Melanie said with a twinkle in her eye. "I know you."

Samantha refrained from arguing or saying anything that might give away more than she was ready to reveal yet.

They went inside together, Melanie smirking and Samantha wondering just how well her sister might know her after all.

Chapter Eighteen

"YOU SURE YOU want to do this?"

Erin picked a stray blue feather from her T-shirt and yanked the legs of her dark wash jeans so they reached the tops of her black Chucks. It was the closest thing to funeral attire that she'd brought with her, considering she'd missed her grandpa's funeral and hadn't planned on anyone else dying while she was in town.

"I'm sure," she said, brushing her hair from her face as a gust of wind whipped across the parking lot. "We'll just go in quietly and hide in the back of the church. You can point and nod at people and help me narrow down who might have also been in my house. Now that we know why Paul was there."

"Why we *assume* Paul was there." Zach stood beside her with his hands in his gray pants pockets, rocking back and forth on his heels. "Still just pissing in the dark with these theories."

"At least we've got a nightlight now."

"You're relentless." Zach shook his head. "And stubborn. And all kinds of other pain-in-the-ass stuff."

"Watch your mouth," she hissed. "I do not want to get struck by lightning sitting next to you."

They followed the flow of people streaming inside the huge front doors of St. Rose Catholic Church. Erin hadn't set foot in this or any other church since her last Sunday with Grandpa. She'd missed a whole bunch of services in the weeks before leaving, but she'd wanted to sit with him in their favorite pew one last time before hitting the road. She'd never realized it would be the *last* last time.

Just before they reached the doors, someone stepped in front of them. Erin almost didn't recognize her without her Lunch Shack shirt or apron and her hair loose. Thick streaks of gray hairs brushed her shoulders and glinted in the sunlight.

"Good morning, Ms. Weaver," Zach chirped.

"Hello, Zachary." Addie's gaze was firmly set on Erin. "I was wondering if I could steal Erin here for a quick chat before we go in."

"Seeing as how I'm not actually her handler, she's free to make that decision herself." Zach looked pretty proud of himself but didn't get the response he'd hoped from Addie. Didn't get any response. After a glance at Erin to make sure she didn't give him their secret *save me* gesture, he said, "I'll wait inside."

A less strong but much longer gust of wind blew between them as Zach turned to leave. This wind was picking up a lot faster than Erin had expected. She really should have checked the weather to see if that storm had changed track.

"What do you need now?" Erin asked. "I promise I'm not here to set anything on fire. Literally *or* figuratively."

Addie glanced over her shoulder to make sure Zach was out of earshot. "I just wanted to thank you for bringing that order to Sergeant Ardoin the other evening."

"Oh." Erin was not expecting that. She'd come in her armor, fully prepared for a barrage of verbal missiles from all directions. Never in a million years did she expect to walk up to a *thank you*. "You're welcome. It was no big deal, really."

"It was a big deal. Or at least it was important. We all care about that girl, and it pains me to my bones to see her hurting like that. That rat bastard of a..." She pressed her lips tight together and did a sign of the cross. "Anyway, thank you. You're about the only one she'd have opened the door for, so thanks for that."

Erin knew she should take the appreciation and walk away. But she had more questions that needed answering today.

She had to know the answer to this one.

"What made you think she'd open the door for me?"

Addie frowned and glanced around. "I saw how she looked at you in that cafe Friday. And how she defended you. I may be stubborn, and a lot of other things, but I know what I saw."

She relaxed and smiled at Erin. It was the first time

Erin had ever seen Addie's teeth aimed at her and not in a snarl.

"For what it's worth," Addie added, "I'm rooting for you two."

"Rooting for... I don't know—"

Addie held up a finger as the church bells rang. "Time to get inside." She patted Erin on the side of the arm. "I'll see you later."

Then Addie spun around and double-timed into the church, leaving Erin alone outside, trying to figure out what the heck had just happened.

Another gust of wind snapped her out of her confusion, and Erin hustled inside where Zach waited.

"What in the world was that about? Addie came in here full-blown grinning. And not a cat-that-ate-the-canary kind of grin. She looked... *happy*. What did you do to her?"

"Nothing," Erin whispered. She looped her arm around Zach's and pulled him toward the pews. "I'll tell you later."

The little church was packed, but Erin spotted a friendly face waving at her near the wall. She dragged Zach with her down the side by the small stained glass windows to the second pew from the rear. Trey scooted so they could sit on the end.

"Do I want to ask how things are going with you?"

She shrugged. "Probably not."

"Figured." Trey leaned forward to nod at Zach. "Hey."

Zach waved and gave an awkward smile across Erin in response.

She looked around the church, sizing up everyone. Making a mental note of who she recognized and remembered and which faces were a complete mystery. She also made note of where people were sitting. Context was everything.

She whispered to Trey, "Which one is that Keller cousin you said was in trouble a lot?"

It was the one lead she hadn't checked up on yet.

He pointed up front. "Third row left. With the rest of them."

And there they were, a whole pew of Kellers. Erin didn't see the head Keller in charge, Samantha's mother, but she did see Samantha's sister, Melanie, and a man she assumed was the sister's husband. Then the brother, Charles or Chad or Chuck. Something like that. She remembered him being in all the nerdy clubs their tiny high school had. He'd gone off to college, and she had no idea why he ever came back to this place.

At the very end of the pew was a young man with ratty blond hair who looked like he'd just woken up and had been dragged out here by one of them. Between the ratty cousin and the preppy brother, a familiar face with a slick dark ponytail turned and fired a friendly warning gaze at the back of the church. Directly at Erin.

The priest passed the Kellers' pew and walked up to the altar, so Samantha returned her attention to the front of the church. But Erin kept her eyes on the woman she'd just been told by Addie might have a thing for her. More than a buzzed self-destructive kiss like Erin had come to assume was at the root of what happened the other night.

That look proved Addie was making up nonsense theories again. As usual.

"Ooh, you're in troooouuuuble," Zach whispered beside her.

For the first time in her life, Erin prayed for a long service.

Chapter Nineteen

WITH TREY AND ZACH FLANKING, Erin filed out of the church. They were accompanied by the town's entire population. Every business down Main Street must have closed for the funeral.

What would this place do if someone who they'd actually liked died? Would they shut down the whole town for a solid week?

Her heart clenched, realizing she could have had the answer to those exact questions if she'd come home after Grandpa died.

Home.

Was she calling it that again?

When they stepped away from the crowd and into the open parking lot, a hard gust hit, sending her hair flying in Trey's face. "I swear that wind picked up while we were in there."

Zach nodded in agreement. "Need to secure some things around both our houses. Ready to head out?"

Erin debated running off with Zach before the tall, obviously annoyed but still stunning brunette headed their way reached them. Erin might be short, but she could sprint to Zach's truck in a hurry.

"I probably need to deal with this first."

"Want me to give you a ride?" Trey asked. "Office is shut down for the day, so I can hang around and drop you off when you're ready to go."

"Thanks. That would be great, if you don't mind."

"Not at all."

"Alrighty," Zach said. "I'll get a jump start on my place, then we can prep yours soon as you get back." He squeezed her forearm gently. "Good luck. Later, man."

He and Trey waved goodbye, and Zach headed toward his truck. Trey tried to slip away, but not before Samantha reached them.

"Hey, Trey. How's it going?"

"Pretty good. You?"

"I'll survive."

Not the confident kind of response Erin had grown to expect from Samantha over the last few days. It was a little heartbreaking.

Trey cleared his throat and pointed at absolutely no one. "Oh, look. A person I know and should say hello to." He patted Erin on the shoulder. "I'll catch up with you in a bit. Good to see you, Sam."

"You, too," said Samantha.

Erin just shook her head. He hadn't even bothered to play that smooth.

She pressed her lips together, struggling for the right

thing to say here. Finally, she settled on, "I didn't cause any trouble. Proud of me?"

Samantha gave a sad frown. "Sorry about that. I'm under a lot of stress. And pressure. And scrutiny. I panicked, and my brain went to worst-case scenarios. I shouldn't have projected that on you."

Erin could only blink. This day was just full of things she hadn't expected.

Maybe Addie had been on the right track earlier, after all.

"Actually, I was going to apologize for snapping at you," Erin said. "I've given you and everyone around here plenty of reason to believe I'm capable of stirring up mess."

"But you didn't."

"No, I did not." Erin grinned. She couldn't hide her absolute delight around Samantha, even if she wanted to. "So did you get the evidence from Officer what's-his-name?"

"It's waiting for me at the station. I haven't been in yet today." Lines settled in on her forehead. "I needed to do my storm prep first. This thing's picking up fast, and I didn't want to be caught at work later without having done anything."

"Do you need a hand? Zach and I can go over to help."

"No, it's fine. I think I've got everything taken care of now."

But it didn't look fine. In fact, Samantha looked the opposite of everything being taken care of.

"What is it then? I thought the storm wasn't supposed to get much stronger."

"It isn't. I'm just not looking forward to having to take Dexter to my Mom's. My sister stays there during storms, and I used to leave him with Nathan. My property floods sometimes. The house is raised enough, but the water can be impassible for a couple days. I'm afraid to leave him home and have him stuck where I can't get to him." Her frown deepened. "But I really don't want to deal with my mother, either."

Erin could understand that. It was also reassuring to hear that Samantha wasn't excited to spend more time with her family. It reassured Erin that Samantha wasn't buying into all her mother's family legacy bull-crap like Erin had feared.

Another gust blew across them, and Erin had to peel her hair out of her mouth. "Would he stay with me? You can bring him over this afternoon. I'd be glad to hang out with him." She paused, her heart racing. "You can both stay. I've got plenty of room in that house."

"Oh, you don't have to—"

"It'll be fine. You know Zach's gonna show up anyway, so it'll be like a big ol' slumber party. With a dog. And a parrot."

Samantha laughed. "Sounds fun."

She bit her lip, and Erin wanted to grab her and kiss her right there in front of half the town and the priest shaking hands behind them.

"Don't think about it. Just bring Dexter. And snacks if you have them."

With a smirk, Samantha said, "You didn't go to the store, did you?"

"What do you think?"

"At least I can feel like I'm helping out this way," Samantha said. "I'll bring snacks and Dexter in a little while."

"Good. I'll see you then."

Erin waved awkwardly as Samantha wove through parked cars to her own. Trey rejoined her a few seconds later.

"And what exactly is your gigantic smile for?"

"Nothing."

"Liar."

"I'm just really excited about storm snacks." Erin pulled her attention from Samantha and redirected it to Trey. "Speaking of storm snacks. You should hang out with us through this thing. Zack is staying at the house, too."

"Thanks. Sounds fun, but I want to stay at our place. Mom and Dad have been through their fair share of these, but I'd worry too much if I'm not around."

"I get it." Erin bumped against his arm. "We'll have to do a non-storm sleepover for all of us another day."

Trey laughed. "That sounds dangerous."

"Does that mean you're in on a rain check?"

Trey's big, dark eyes stared into Erin's for longer than was probably necessary to answer that question. She got the distinct feeling that he was as glad and surprised as she was to have found friends in this place after all this time.

That charming grin made its way back to his face. "You bet."

Samantha stacked all of Paul's case files and began stuffing them in a bright blue tote bag that said "Pug Life" with a sketch of what could have been Dexter's twin.

She'd originally planned to ride out the storm at the station, since it was a better option than spending a night with no power at her mother's house. There wasn't enough wine in all of Etta to make that even remotely bearable.

But then Erin had offered an alternative. A mighty enticing alternative.

Now she could spend the night going through her files in light of the new evidence. She'd be on call through the storm, and the plan was for her to take any emergency calls in Erin's area, while Dustin tackled the area near his mom's house and Gary ran point at the station. It was a tactical bonus.

Plus, she'd get to ride out the storm all night with Erin.

And Zach and Dexter and that parrot.

But mostly Erin.

"Dustin, where'd you put those prescriptions you bagged from the Sonnier house?"

"They're on your desk," he said, pouring a cup of coffee.

"Um, no. They're not. Did you maybe put them down somewhere on the way to my desk?" She lifted the files, one folder at a time, checking underneath and inside each. No luck.

"No." He walked over and moved a stack of papers secured with a binder clip. "I put the bags right here last night."

"Connie, did you see some evidence bags on my desk?"

Maybe Gary had asked her to bring them in his office to keep them in there. As soon as he got off his phone call, she could grab them for a second. She wanted to take a look before she headed out to make note of the doctor and see how many prescriptions they'd found. Maybe she could be on the lookout for more at Erin's place while she was there. They could have a scavenger hunt sleepover.

She really was turning into a giddy teenager.

This was all Erin's doing. And Samantha wasn't entirely sure she didn't like this change in herself. It felt kind of nice to be genuinely excited about something for once.

Could she really become a person who was excited about hanging out with people? Better yet, a person who actually had fun?

"They were there when I came in," Connie said. "And I'm pretty sure I saw them when I left for the funeral."

That pit made a reappearance in Samantha's gut. She did not have a good feeling about this.

"Did anyone besides us come through here this

morning? Did you lock up before you left for the funeral?"

"No, Chief stayed here," she said. "We were going to go to the service together, but…" She paused to frown. "His meeting with Deputy Fonseca ran late, so he told me I should go ahead to the funeral without him."

The pit in Samantha's stomach widened.

This really did not smell good. Not. At. All.

Samantha's brain scrambled for a plan. She didn't want to alert Connie or Dustin that she was suspicious of Jordan. Not yet, at least.

"I'm sure he's holding it in his office, then. I'll just check base with him on it later. There's enough to keep me busy here." She patted her bag of files and lifted the straps onto her shoulder. "I'm gonna head out and grab Dexter before things get too dicey. Y'all stay safe tonight!"

Connie and Dustin both wished her the same, hollering at her back as she hurried out of the door and down the street.

Panic and conspiracy theories ran amok through her head as she sprinted to her car. All her excitement about the upcoming evening blew away with the wind gust rushing down Main Street.

Chapter Twenty

ERIN FOLDED the last of the freshly washed towels and placed the stack on their shelf in the hall bathroom. Her clothes were in the dryer now, so all the laundry was clean in case they lost power for a few days. Despite Zach's nagging, Erin decided that was all the cleaning she planned to do ahead of this storm.

She joined Trey and Zach on the porch to see how they were doing with the outside prep.

"That's the last of them." Trey wiped his forehead and took off his gloves. "I'd better head out."

"You sure we can't convince you to stay?" Erin asked. "Sam said she might have plans for a scavenger hunt now."

"A *murder* scavenger hunt? Trapped here during a storm?" He curled his lip. "That sounds more like some escape room junk. No, thanks."

"Chicken?" Zach teased.

"No, I just prefer non-murdery slumber parties is all."

He smiled and handed the gloves to Zach. "If you guys are all set, I've gotta help Dad with a couple more things at our place."

"Thanks for all your help here," said Erin. She could have handled putting up the boards with Zach herself, but Trey and Zach took care of everything much faster than she ever could. They turned out to be a well-oiled storm prep machine. "And thanks for the ride home."

"No problem." Trey waved to them both as he got in his car. "Holler if y'all need. Be safe!"

"You, too!" Zach shouted over the engine. After the car backed out of the long gravel driveway, he said, "He seems all right."

Erin gave him a sideways glance, similar to the ones he'd given her over the last few days.

"Nope," Zach said. "Still straight."

"Just checking." Erin grinned as the car drove off down the road. "I like him, too."

Zach smacked the gloves together in a clap. "What's next on the list?"

"I don't know, you tell me."

It had been a long time since she'd had to do any of this. And she'd never had to figure it out on her own. She only did whatever Grandpa had asked. Thankfully, Zach knew where all the boards were and had helped Grandpa over the last couple of years, so that part was covered.

"I know you went through storms in New Orleans," Zach said.

"The last time I went through one of these, my job

was to pick the Netflix series to binge and make sure we had enough wine. Renting in the city has its benefits."

"How are you on laundry?"

"Towels are done. Just a load of clothes left drying."

She was learning that storm prep was kind of a scam. It was just a way to make people clean their houses when they had a lot of nervous anticipation and not much else to do.

"Anything you want to cook before the power goes out? Anything we can't grill later? I brought eggs."

She wrinkled her nose. "Eggs?"

"Yeah, eggs. They'll go bad if the power's out too long, and you can't eat 'em raw. We can boil them before the power goes out, then we can keep 'em in the ice chest."

"I don't really like the idea of a house full of people on a diet of boiled eggs."

"You'll like it more when you're looking for easy protein in the mornings."

"I thought this thing wasn't supposed to be that bad?"

"Habits," he said.

But something was bugging him.

"What?" Erin asked. "It's not picking up, is it?"

The worst was waiting to see if one of these things that was supposed to be nothing blew up right before it hit the coast in the middle of the night. So much about these storms was unpredictable. She'd never had to worry about it before, but now she had to not only keep herself safe, but also a bird and a house and her guests.

She was turning into a responsible person she hardly recognized. With Zach's assistance, of course. She'd still be the complete screw-up everyone expected if she'd be on her own through this. But she did want to make sure everyone staying with her was safe there.

"No," he frowned. "Opposite. It's slowing down."

"That's good though, right? The outer bands are moving over land, so shouldn't be too much worse, I thought."

They'd turned on the TV for weather updates while they went through the house prepping. It had a name now. Tropical Storm Tristan. But it wasn't even a category one hurricane. Not yet, at least.

"Right," Zach said. "But now they're worried it might stall out over us and dump a whole bunch of rain."

"Isn't rain better than wind?"

"It is if you don't flood."

She looked around the house at Grandpa's stuff *everywhere*. Lord help them if they had to pick up everything off the floor. "But it doesn't usually flood here at the house, right?"

"Right. We should be fine." He gave a tight smile. "I'm glad you convinced Sam to come here. Her road floods bad. And most of town will be waterlogged for a few days after. Might make getting power back on tricky. So what we've got here supply-wise is what we've got. Maybe for a week if this thing doesn't move out."

Erin tried not to panic. "A week? I'm guessing runs to Addie's will be out of the question."

He snapped his fingers. "Good call. I've got bacon at

my house. We can cook it while we boil the eggs, then tomorrow I'll make you the second-best BLT you've ever had."

"Now you're talking."

"I'm gonna run back and grab it. Might as well clear out the fridge and freezer anyway, in case the road does flood, and we can't get to my place tomorrow. Even if the power's out here, we'll have meat in the ice chest to grill."

She pointed at the big chest nearby on the porch. "I thought that thing was full of beer."

He winked before heading down the steps. "I expect to make room in it by morning!"

"I'm not holding your hair tonight!" she shouted at him while he revved up his old truck.

Erin was about to shut the door when she spotted a blue Honda easing around Zach's truck on the gravel driveway.

Her heart fluttered.

Fluttered.

She was not a flutterer.

But as the car stopped in front of the porch and Samantha got out and waved to her, Erin's heart felt like a cage for a thousand tiny butterflies flapping their wings against the chamber walls. Samantha was wearing a plain black T-shirt and bootcut jeans with hiking shoes, and it was the first time Erin had seen her with her hair down. Her straight, dark hair fell over her shoulders, with long layered bangs framing her face.

"Need a hand?" Erin skipped down the steps and practically ran to the open car door.

Samantha had a confused-looking Dexter tucked in one arm and handed Erin a plastic grocery bag filled with dog food, treat bags, and bowls. "Thanks. Let's get him in and settled first, then I'll come back for the food and stuff."

"Snacks?"

"The junkiest of junk food."

"Oh, thank goodness," Erin sighed. "I thought we were going to have nothing but boiled eggs for the night."

Samantha grabbed a dog bed and blanket with her free hand and shut the door with her hip. "Ew, what? Why?"

"Zach is apparently some kind of super-efficient prepper," she explained. "But he's bringing bacon now, and he's been really helpful, so I'm making an allowance for the egg-fest."

"Sounds fair."

Erin shut the door behind Samantha, and they were greeted by a chipper, "Hiiiiiiii," from Marty. Erin had been nervous about how he'd react to the strangers, especially the dog, given how he'd lost his tiny bird mind when the officer came to collect the evidence last night. But he seemed as smitten with the little black pug as Erin was with the dog's owner.

Dexter, however, did not share the bird's affection.

The second Samantha placed the dog on the ground,

he ran in circles, barking beneath the birdcage. Erin and Samantha exchanged a silent, *Oh crap*, look.

"Pretty bird!" Marty squawked as he puffed up and spread his wings in an attempt to make a better impression.

No such luck. Dexter remained unimpressed.

Samantha picked him up, but Dexter continued to bark, now with a better view of the offending bird.

"Bring him in here." Erin gestured for them to follow her down the hall. "The two of you can have Grandpa's room. As far as you can get in this house from Zach and his eggs."

"Perfect." Samantha followed with Dexter in one arm and his doggy bed in the other. "Thanks for letting us crash with you. I'll probably head out to patrol a bit once the eye's over us, then after it's completely through, and I'll feel so much better knowing he's safe with people and not stranded where I can't get to him. Or worse. With my mother."

Samantha smiled, recovering quickly from the mention of her mother, but that smile didn't reach her eyes.

"Is something else wrong?" Erin asked.

"No, this room is great." When Erin didn't buy that answer and waited for more, Samantha added, "It's just the case."

"New lead?" Erin wasn't sure how much to push or how much to let on that she had her targets set on Sam's own cousin as a suspect.

"More of a new wrinkle." Samantha shook her head.

"I can't really talk about it, but maybe you could show me where you found those prescriptions later?"

"Of course."

"Thanks."

"So. The tour." Erin pointed to the master bathroom. "You have your own bathroom with a sink for Dexter's water and plenty of places to store his food."

"So he won't pig out and eat through the bag and swallow all his storm food in one night. Good thinking."

"I can't promise the same for me and the junk food, though. I'm a stress eater."

"Good thing I planned ahead and stocked up before the stores closed. I think I bought every weird flavor potato chip. I don't stress eat so much as stress shop."

"Then we make a perfect team." Erin flinched in horror as she realized what she'd just said. "I didn't mean—"

Samantha held up a hand and took a step closer. "It's fine." That thin, crooked smile made another appearance. "And I happen to agree."

Erin reached out and took Sam's hand, then pulled her even closer until their bodies touched. She slipped her free hand around Sam's waist and held her tight against her, with the heat kicking up between them.

When their lips met, Erin forgot all about storms and junk food and dead guys. She could only think about the breathtaking woman whose mouth was against hers. Whose tongue brushed against her lips. Who Erin felt quite sure she could kiss for the rest of the storm, maybe even the rest of her life, and never grow bored or restless.

After a lifetime of restless, she never imagined kissing a *cop* of all people could cure her of that feeling.

"McFlyyyyyyy!!!!"

Marty was the worst doorbell ever.

Announcing Zach's return, she assumed.

"Dang it, Marty."

Samantha laughed and touched her forehead to Erin's. "Is he going to do that all night?"

"Jeez, I hope not." Erin kissed her again, greedy for more kisses. Greedy for more of all of this woman. "If he does, I'm letting Dexter have him."

Chapter Twenty-One

SAMANTHA HANDED Erin two grocery bags filled with chips, granola bars, Pop-Tarts, and all the fruits and vegetables from her fridge. That last part only amounted to the last two satsumas from her tree, three green bananas, four cucumbers, a bell pepper, and one Jazz apple they'd have to fight her to the death for. She loved those things. Which was why there was only one left when she'd stocked up just two days ago.

As she dug in the trunk for the last of the bags, Zach pulled in beside her and walked over with a couple bags of his own.

"Bacon and eggs are here," he said. "Plus some pork fingers that'll work on the pit."

"Great." Samantha held up the remaining bag of toilet paper and paper towels. "Just in case."

Erin shook her head and smiled at them. "What would I do without you two?"

That smile made Samantha prouder than any A on a

test paper ever had. She knew Erin well enough to know she probably didn't prep for this storm, and Samantha was glad she could help. Or at least earn Erin's hospitality during this brief stay.

"Apparently you'd have been wiping your butt with birdcage paper." Zach froze a few steps later. "How are you on birdseed?"

"Good, I think?" Erin cringed. "I have no idea how much that thing eats, but based on the last couple days, I think there's enough for a week or so. I hope."

Zach continued across the gravel and up the steps to the house. "Should be fine. I stocked up not long before you got back."

"Again, thanks," Erin said. "Both of you. You're lifesavers."

"I just brought beer and bacon."

"You're right," said Erin. "Sam and her toilet paper are the real heroes here."

Samantha puffed with pride. She'd rolled up to save the day enough times and been the beneficiary of enough thank-you-cakes that being a toilet paper hero shouldn't feel quite this satisfying. And yet, she'd never felt so useful in her entire life.

They placed the bags on the kitchen counter and began emptying their contents. All except the toilet paper and paper towels, which Erin insisted should stay in the bag and be for emergency use only. She said it was only fair that Samantha should take those back home with her if they weren't needed by the time this was all over and done with.

"Sweet." Zach grabbed the box of Velveeta and a can of Ro-tel. He put them beside the microwave, then pulled a large glass bowl from a nearby cabinet. "Cheese dip time!"

Samantha normally didn't keep the stuff around. No point making a big batch of dip for a party of one. But she'd bought the ingredients, figuring it would be a hit with these two.

Erin put a hand on her stomach. "I haven't had that in years. Yes! Heat that up!"

Zach aimed a large spoon at her. "Don't get bossy." He changed the direction of the spoon to point down the hall. "Now get out of this kitchen and let me work."

"Yes, sir." Erin saluted with a grin.

"McFly!"

"Ugh, Marty," Erin growled. "Enough."

The storm had them all on edge. Marty especially. But Samantha noticed Erin's patience with the bird's noise was also dwindling.

"The vet was talking about some study the other day," Zack said, while he diced cheese. "Apparently, just hearing birds boosts your mood or something. For like eight hours."

Erin rolled her eyes dramatically. "Surely they didn't mean Marty."

"I don't know," Samantha said. "I feel like I'm in a better mood around him."

Never mind that being around Marty meant she was also around Erin. That seemed a key element in this particular equation.

Marty aside, Samantha couldn't remember the last time she felt this happy. Especially with a group of people. The only gatherings she made time for were family dinners or holidays. Those gatherings felt more like work. But with Zach and Erin, this was more like what a family should feel like.

Here, with these two, Samantha's shoulders relaxed a little. She felt like she could be herself here. No walls up. No playing a role. She was just... Samantha.

Erin put a hand on Samantha's and nodded her head toward the hall. "Want me to show you that bookcase?"

"Bookcase?" She was still swimming in good family vibes and didn't want to come up for air. But she'd follow Erin and her smile anywhere.

"That's where I found the prescriptions," Erin said. "And a whole lot of other junk."

"Sure. That would be great."

More than great.

It was the reason Samantha had been able to justify staying here through the storm. She *wanted* to stay here for a bunch of other reasons, so checking out the scene of the crime and the evidence she hadn't been able to see for herself made a great excuse.

Especially since that evidence was now missing.

Samantha ignored that pit in her stomach and followed Erin down the hall into the late Mr. Sonnier's bedroom, where Samantha was riding out the storm. Dexter met them at the door with a flurry of yaps, but he settled once Samantha picked him up and shushed him.

When she returned him to the floor, he scurried off to

lie down in his bed, and Samantha met Erin in front of her grandfather's overflowing but meticulously organized bookshelves.

"You found them stuffed in here?"

"Yes, but more importantly..." Erin pulled out a book, showing Samantha the cover. *The Colour of Magic* by Terry Pratchett. Then she opened it, revealing a neatly carved hole in the middle section of the pages.

"Oh, wow!"

"Yup," said Erin. "They were all stuffed in here. Which explains why Paul didn't find them, even if he'd had plenty of time to look before he was murdered. Grandpa loved his books, but he loved thinking he was clever even more."

"But why would your grandfather hide his unused prescriptions?" Samantha realized she had never asked a very important question for an answer she would have known if she'd had a chance to look at that evidence before it walked off her desk. "How many prescriptions are we talking about?"

Erin's eyes grew wide. "A *lot*. More than anyone should need." She chuckled. "Or that insurance would pay for."

"Why would he have so many if he wasn't filling them or taking the meds?"

"I have no idea," Erin said. "His medicine cabinet is practically empty. Regular anti-inflammatories and over-the-counter stomach stuff. Supplements in the kitchen for achy joints. That's all. From everything he told me on our calls, he was in good health up until the heart attack."

There was an extra weight to Erin's last statement. Guilt, if Samantha had to guess. As much as Erin hated this town, Samantha knew what her grandfather had meant to her. Not knowing what was going on with him and how he landed in the middle of all this was probably eating her up.

"Do you remember what the prescriptions you found were for?"

Erin hesitated, maintaining eye contact. It was clear she didn't want to say whatever was about to come out of her mouth.

"Oxycodone." Erin frowned. "Some brand I didn't recognize, but I looked it up."

Samantha's chest tightened like someone had gripped a fist around her heart. This whole situation had a stink to it, but she didn't want to jump to conclusions.

"I thought you said he was healthy."

"As far as I knew. I mean, he could have been hiding a diagnosis. And it would be like Grandpa to 'tough it out.' But I don't know if he'd hide something that big. Someone around here would have known if he had a big surgery or cancer, even if I didn't."

Samantha heard the pain in those last few words.

"Maybe it wasn't something new. Maybe he had an old injury?"

"Then why keep going to the doctor if he didn't plan on taking anything for the pain?" Erin shook her head. "And they were all recent prescriptions. All within the last several months. Too many for a minor issue."

Samantha frowned. "Unless..."

Erin nodded. "Unless."

Samantha had been hoping to find some reasonable explanation for all of this. Something that made all her fears and suspicions vanish.

Erin stared at the book in her hand. "I thought that stuff was going off the market."

Samantha shook her head. She'd kept up on the court case because she knew prescriptions of all kinds turned street drugs were a problem for lots of communities. A problem that shouldn't be solved by punishing the people who were lied to about the pills and then cut off by overreactive doctors and lawmakers. She wanted to keep current with the issue so her department could help people get the resources they needed, not throw them in jail.

"The big company that lied about their product got in trouble, but the medicine isn't inherently evil," Samantha explained. "People still need the pills, so generic and other brands are available. But overprescribing for profit is always a problem."

And a potential motive.

But there was still a missing piece. Mr. Sonnier's prescriptions didn't draw a direct line to Nathan. Yet. Since Mr. Sonnier hadn't filled them, the only person potentially on the hook so far was the doctor. The prescriptions that were now missing.

That, unfortunately, painted a giant flashing arrow

pointed at either her boss or her political opponent. Or both. They were the last people in the office when the evidence went missing. One or both of them could have made that evidence disappear.

Samantha's money was on Jordan. Not just because she didn't want to imagine the chief involved in this, or because she couldn't stand Jordan Fonseca, but because Jordan was the only one with a connection and possible motive.

Had Nathan been worried about the evidence tying him to the doctor and asked Jordan to make it disappear as payment for securing his win in the election?

It sounded far-fetched, but she couldn't ignore the connections. Nor could she ignore the fact that it sounded exactly like something Nathan and Jordan would do.

"I don't get it," Samantha said. "Why would he keep them in here? Why go through the trouble of hiding them in a book?"

"He kept everything of value here." Erin held up a finger and grabbed a book on the second shelf. She pointed at the spine, which read, *The Collective Stories of Raymond Carver*. Then she opened the cover, once again revealing a hole in the pages. This time, filled with cash. "See? Carver. Ca- for *cash*."

Samantha knew Erin's grandfather had always been mildly eccentric, but this was more than she'd expected. "Are all the books like this?"

"No," Erin said. "Some are just normal books. I haven't been through all of them yet."

Meaning they could be standing in front of more evidence.

"Wait. If he kept his valuables here..."

Erin nodded. "He considered those prescriptions valuable."

"But why? If he wasn't filling them, what was their value to him?"

Erin waited silently while Samantha pondered the possibilities. Something in her eyes told Samantha that Erin had an inkling of an answer to her question, but she was waiting for Samantha to figure it out on her own.

"Maybe they weren't valuable to *him* specifically."

They were valuable, Samantha had to admit. Street value for one. But also to her and the department for protecting the parish.

"Wait, you can't think your grandfather was on some kind of Nancy Drew mission."

"No, I think everyone in this town knew the truth already, so he wasn't solving a mystery." Erin paused, biting her lip for a second, then continuing. "I think he might have been on a mission to take them all down. *Everyone* involved."

"Everyone," Samantha repeated.

Everyone meant the doctor *and* whoever was filling those prescriptions. The only pharmacy in Etta and its only pharmacist.

Nathan.

"So what's Paul's connection to all of this?" Samantha was thinking through this out loud, the same way she worked through so many of her cases with the chief or Dustin. She shouldn't have been discussing these details with Erin, but she needed to work it out, and this was the only way she knew how.

"What's Paul's connection to the doctor?" Erin asked. "Or... you know who."

"I'm assuming Trey filled you in on Paul's disability?" Erin nodded.

"He was hooked on prescription painkillers. Oxy, when the company was in its prime. That wasn't a secret. Same doctor on the edge of town, I'd guess. Some doctor from out of state who set up shop in an area they knew had a lot of oil field injuries and disabilities needing pain management. Except, instead of helping manage, they used them as cash cows. We've tried to shut them down for years with no solid ground to build a case on. No one wants to snitch and lose their supplier. Even with the Sacklers out of business, some of the pill mill doctors have contracts with other brands now, from what I understand. Just shifted instead of shutting down."

"Makes sense," Erin said. "So Paul wouldn't have been working with Grandpa to take down his own doctor."

Samantha shrugged. "He was also pretty angry about his situation. And impulsive. But no, I don't see your grandfather involving him."

"Maybe he just knew Grandpa had the prescriptions and was trying to steal them? Wrong place, wrong time?"

"That seems more likely."

But then there was that part about Paul's car not

being at the scene. How did he plan to steal them and get out in a hurry without a vehicle?

Erin's expression deflated. "But that leaves us back with no murderer and no motive."

Us.

Samantha decided to let the word slip by uncommented upon. Pointing it out might blow it away like a wisp of smoke.

Besides. She'd never admit it to anyone, but she liked the idea of working together with Erin. Being partners. Even for this one stormy night.

As if on cue, the old house rattled and shook with a gust of wind.

"The bands are getting closer together. And stronger."

"We should be fine here," Erin said. "This house has stood through a lot worse."

A lot worse, like a murder.

But Samantha knew Erin meant storms. The winds on this thing would be nothing compared to some of the storms that had passed through over the last several decades. They were safe inside.

Safe inside a crime scene.

"So Paul was here to score easy access to drugs."

It was clear Erin wouldn't let this go. Samantha could relate, and it was downright endearing. Erin hadn't even wanted to be in this town to begin with, but had an overwhelming need to solve a crime. Like a grown-up Veronica Mars who wasn't getting paid.

"The question is," Erin continued, "who killed Paul and why?"

"That is the big question."

"Another addict?"

Samantha frowned. "Not if we consider the manner in which they killed him."

"Right," Erin said. "Subtle. Not sloppy or heat of the moment. Someone who had access to whatever was in that needle."

Which put them right back with the doctor or pharmacist.

Samantha had a sinking suspicion that if she hadn't tanked this election herself the other night, solving this case would do it. Because she was about to put herself directly in Nathan's cross-hairs.

"Do you think he could have killed someone?" Erin's voice was small and gentle. Questioning without judgment. "You know him better than anyone. Do you really think he has it in him?"

Erin wasn't wrong. Samantha probably knew Nathan better than anyone else in this town. But that didn't mean she actually knew the man. He would *never* let anyone know the real Nathan. But she caught glimpses. And she eventually learned to read through his lies and manipulation. Not completely, but better.

"No, not by his own hands," she said. "But I think he'd encourage someone else to take care of a problem for him."

"Encourage?"

"Pay. Bribe. Blackmail. Something that would make a slightly less direct connection to him."

"That makes sense," Erin said. "For him."

"Now the only question is, who connects the dots? Paul was about to get his hands on those prescriptions. Nathan wanted them gone, and Paul was in the way. Who did Nathan send to do his dirty work?"

"Who did he have dirt on or who needed money?" Erin asked. "Or who had their own stake in keeping this doctor prescribing pills?"

Samantha chuckled. "Half the town falls under that first question."

Then she remembered why they were looking at a bunch of books and not the evidence itself. She knew she should keep this bit quiet, but she needed someone else to confirm that she wasn't overreacting out of professional jealousy or some other petty reason.

"I think Jordan could be helping him. He might not have murdered Paul himself, but I think he's up to his neck in this."

Erin stared wide-eyed for a few moments, then shook her head. "Wait. Jordan Fonseca? *Deputy* Fonseca?"

"The one and only."

"Why would he want Paul dead?" Erin shook her head again. "Wait, do you think *he* was after the prescriptions, too?"

"No, but I'm afraid he's involved in covering for Nathan." Samantha frowned. This part hurt the most, no matter how much she tried to pretend she didn't care. "I'm pretty sure Nathan's backing his campaign."

Erin's shock transformed into white-hot fury as her eyes narrowed and her hands balled into fists. "That rat bastard."

"Among many other things, yes. You won't get an argument from me on that."

"I don't remember anything much about Jordan, since he was older than me."

Erin tilted her head in thought. It was so cute Samantha had to fight the urge to take the woman's face in her hands and pick up where they'd left off earlier. If they hadn't been discussing a murder in this very house.

"Do you think Jordan has it in him?" Erin asked.

"I don't think so, but I can't rule it out." With a nod toward the bedroom door, Samantha said, "We should probably check on Zach and that dip. I think better with food."

Samantha could stay in that room with Erin all night, but she needed time to process everything before she connected the next set of dots.

Erin winked. "Me, too. Plus, we don't want to leave Zach alone in the kitchen too long. He'll wipe out all the snacks before this storm gets halfway through."

As Samantha followed Erin out of the bedroom, Zach and snacks were the last things on her mind.

Chapter Twenty-Two

ZACK AND ERIN picked up their cards as Samantha slid the pennies from the center into her ever-growing pile. She was whooping both of their butts, despite claiming she hadn't played bourré in years.

Erin was skilled at the game itself, but since she'd grown up playing with her grandfather, she'd never mastered betting strategy.

Zach, on the other hand, had boasted about his bourré mastery all day leading up to their game. He'd brought his "best" deck and a gallon plastic bag filled with pennies for them to use as chips. Despite all that, he was clearly the worst player of the trio.

The house shook around them as a howl roared past the window near Erin. The glass rattled, and she instinctively looked over her shoulder, knowing it was boarded up and she couldn't see outside.

Hurricane Tristan had crept closer all day, but the winds had intensified quickly over the past half hour.

While she was grateful Grandpa didn't have any big trees close enough to fall on them, she wasn't used to being out in the open like this in a storm anymore. The house was raised off the ground and older than all of them put together.

"We're fine," Zach reminded her in his soothing tenor. "Sam, I think it's your turn."

Marty squawked in protest as a big gust rattled the house. Not a fan of this storm any more than Erin was.

Samantha's phone rang beside her. When she picked it up, Erin played a card while simultaneously craning her neck to catch a glimpse of the caller.

Not that it was any of her business.

Somehow, she'd loosened up around Zach and Samantha this evening. *Somehow* being a bunch of her grandfather's gin from the back of the cabinet. Probably the same bottle she used to sneak sips out of on Saturday nights.

Her grandfather's bourbon was long gone, though. It had served its purpose, fueling a notorious shed fire.

"Hey, Chief. Problem?"

Samantha had snapped into business mode, and somehow it was sexy as hell.

That dang gin again.

That gin *and* those jeans wrapped tight around Sam's hips and thighs.

A frown settled in deep on Sam's face. "I was kind of hoping you had them in your office."

Erin and Zach exchanged a look, both shrugging to

let the other know they had no idea what Samantha was talking about.

Samantha looked up at the pair, then said, "I'll be there in five minutes."

"Something wrong?" Zach asked, as Samantha stood and looked around for her keys.

"No," she said. "I just have to get to the station. The chief needs help finding something."

"*Now*?" Erin said. "You can't go out in *this*." She gestured at the boarded-up window as Hurricane Tristan shook the house to emphasize the point.

Samantha grabbed her keys from the dinette table. "Sorry to break up the party. Is it okay if Dexter stays here? I'll be back later. Just need to check on something real quick."

"Dexter's fine." Something was wrong. Erin didn't know what, but something had Samantha spooked. "I'll go with you. You shouldn't go out in this alone. Zach can stay here with Dexter. Right?"

"Uh, yeah. Sure. More snacks for me," Zach said. "But should either of you be going out in this? Storm's still a Cat 1."

"No." Sam's voice snapped with a sharpness that cut through Erin and stopped her in her tracks. "I need to go alone."

Erin's face stung with the cutting tone of Samantha's words.

The gin swirled in her brain, feeding her memories of her previous conversations with Samantha and her family and not being ready to reveal certain parts of herself.

Hiding out here during a storm with Dexter was fine. Kissing on her front porch in the middle of nowhere was also fine. Being seen together in public? Clearly not fine.

Whether it was because Erin was the town screw-up or Samantha wasn't ready to be seen with a woman—any woman—it didn't matter. It added up to the same thing.

"Need to go alone?" Erin asked. "Or don't want to be seen there with me?"

Samantha's eyes softened, and Erin briefly doubted her conclusion.

"It's not that."

The gin continued to swirl Erin's thoughts like an out-of-control blender. "Are you sure?"

After a much too long pause, Samantha said, "It's about the case. I have to talk to him alone."

"Why now? It's not safe. And why can't this be a phone call?"

Despite all of their conversations, Samantha was still trying to fix everything and save everyone on her own. Erin thought they were moving past that. They'd looked at those bookshelves together, and Samantha had talked through what they knew with her. They'd felt like a bit of a team back there.

Erin froze.

If Samantha wasn't embarrassed to be seen with her—a fact Erin's reactive brain wasn't convinced of but that the rest of her more rational thoughts were willing to give the benefit of the doubt on—then there was some bit of news or evidence she didn't want Erin to find out about.

"Unless you know something you haven't told us."

Samantha's mouth tightened. "I don't know anything yet."

"But you suspect something. Something you don't want me to know about." Erin felt a stab in her heart as the reactive gin thoughts won their battle against rationality. "Are you *covering* for whoever killed my grandpa? Is that it?"

"Erin, no."

"Kellers protect Kellers, is that it?" Erin felt a sickening pit open in her stomach. "Or is it a different family you're protecting?"

Samantha looked like she'd been slapped, and Erin immediately regretted the accusation. But only for a moment. Because Samantha didn't deny it.

"We can talk about it when I get back," Samantha said as she left.

The door closed behind her, leaving Erin standing in the middle of the living room and Zach still sitting on the carpet with the cards. Even Marty was silent.

After a long while, Zach said, "Erin?"

She shook her head. There was nothing to say. Nothing she wanted to talk about.

Either Samantha was covering for her family and Erin had completely misjudged her character and her loyalty to them, or she didn't want to be seen with Erin.

Neither was an option Erin wanted to discuss.

She'd been right all along about this place. She didn't belong here. Samantha had been the only person aside from Zach who she'd thought really accepted her. Understood her. Was glad to have her around. She didn't come back here to be someone's secret or feel ashamed of who she was or have someone she'd grown to care about choose their shitty family over her.

Erin had left all of this behind once before. She could do it again.

Zach collected the cards in a pile. "You all right?"

"I will be."

"Wanna play something else?"

"Not really."

She plopped onto the couch and grabbed the remote. The moment the TV switched on, a loud pop sounded outside and the lights went out. If they'd been able to see out the window, they probably would have witnessed a bright flash as a tree branch fell on a power line. But the boards had blocked the light show, and now they were in complete darkness.

Erin sighed. "I was going to suggest we watch something while we still had power."

"Was hoping it wouldn't go out for a few more hours." Zach turned on the battery-powered lantern and set it in the center of the room. "Deal you in? Your pick of game."

Erin slid to the floor beside him. She didn't have anything better to do, and she sure as hell didn't want to sit in the dark with her thoughts. "Gin. The game to go with my drinks. Which I'm done with, by the way. The drink, I mean. And I'm tired of beating you in bourré."

Zach shuffled the deck and winked at her. "Cheer up."

"Cheer up?"

Zach was coming dangerously close to getting thrown out in this weather. She'd rather mope alone than with a Pollyanna through this cursed storm.

"Yup," he said with a shit-eating grin, as he began tossing cards face down, back and forth between them. "You're about to witness an epic ass-whooping."

Erin tried and failed to hold back a laugh. "Just shut up and deal."

Chapter Twenty-Three

ERIN LOST interest in cards after two hands of gin rummy and declined Zach's offer to pick a different game. She'd lost her stomach for kicking his butt.

"So what now?" He gathered the cards into a pile and began scooping his pennies back into the plastic bag.

"What are our options?"

Not that she wanted to do anything right now. The only thing she really wanted to do was get in her car and find Samantha to work this out.

Maybe she'd overreacted.

Probably.

It was kind of her thing.

There must have been some other reason for Samantha's swift and secretive departure. Erin couldn't believe that she would choose to protect Nathan for any reason, but whatever information had Samantha running out in this storm must have had something to do with the case.

And if it didn't point to Nathan, it had to implicate her cousin.

But Samantha had given no sign before this that she'd put her integrity aside to protect a family member. Maybe that sister of hers, but some random cousin?

It didn't make any sense.

"Snacks?"

"I'm not hungry." The thought of eating anything right now made Erin nauseous. She was too upset, and not about the weather.

"Think I remember seeing puzzles around here. Want to start one?" He patted the little lantern beside him. "I've got plenty of batteries for this thing."

"Sure."

Truthfully, she didn't want to do that either, but she needed to do *something*.

Zach handed her the lantern and took the small flashlight with him as he stood. "Get a drink and clear a space. I'll pick a puzzle. Requests?"

"Anything. I trust your puzzle judgment."

Erin went into the kitchen and moved a couple of bags of chips from the table to the counter beside the sink, but she didn't bother making a drink. Her earlier buzz had worn off, and at this point, she'd just end up drinking too much and wallowing. Or follow through on some impulsive whim, like chasing after Samantha in the middle of a hurricane.

Her phone rang, and she felt a little pinch of disappointment when she didn't see Samantha's name on the screen. But once the actual caller registered in her brain, a pit of panic opened up in her stomach.

"Hey, are you guys okay?"

"Yeah, yeah, we're fine," Trey said. "You?"

"Yeah, all good out here, too. Well, Zach and I are good."

"Where's Sam?"

"Ran off to the station to hide some evidence or cover some other way for her cousin or that rat bastard of an ex she's got."

Okay, she really didn't believe either of those, but Erin didn't know what else to think at this point.

Trey was silent for a good long time. So long that when the wind rattled the house again, she thought maybe they lost the cell signal.

Finally, he said, "I don't think either of them murdered Paul."

Erin's back straightened. She hadn't wanted to believe Samantha would really break the law to protect anyone, but she clearly wasn't the only one who had doubts. She didn't know if that made her feel worse or better. "But you think she's covering for someone. Who?"

"Not necessarily." His voice was hesitant. Whatever he was getting at, he didn't like being the one to say it.

"Well, what then?"

"I remembered something. A couple things, but one thing in particular. It might not mean anything, but it's been bugging me all night. Remember when we met for lunch, and you went outside and your tire was slashed?"

216

"How could I forget? You know someone who hates me enough to do that?"

"No, not exactly. But I do remember leaving to meet you and seeing someone near your car. They weren't doing anything, just standing and looking around, and I didn't know your car was there. But I did realize I forgot my phone and went back in to work to grab it. When I came out again, he—"

Trey was quiet again.

"He who?" she asked. "You know who it was?"

More silence.

"Trey?"

She looked at the screen. The call had dropped. She tried to call him back, but the signal was gone.

Zach walked in as she was holding the phone in the air and swinging it around the room, trying to get a signal again. He put a puzzle on the table. It was an illustrated fishing village. Colorful. Lots of little details to make it easier. Good thing, because it was two thousand pieces.

"Cell tower's probably out. Hardly ever happens, but I guess we got lucky this time."

She stared at her phone. Erin knew she should stay put until the storm passed. She should wait for a signal and call Trey back.

But she couldn't sit still for another second. What if whoever slashed her tire was tied to the murder somehow, and Trey might have a missing piece to this whole thing? He might have some clue about the real reason Samantha left and was hiding things from her.

"What are you doing?" Zach asked as she grabbed her keys from the counter.

"Where does Trey live?"

"Out on Benoit Road. Just past Mr. Fontenot's farm," he said. "What's wrong? Are they okay?"

"Yeah, I think so. He was about to tell me something before the signal cut out. He sounded upset."

"Wait, I'll come with you." He reached to shut off the lantern.

"No, you stay here. Please. Keep an eye on the place and let Sam in if she gets back before me."

He didn't look happy with that. "Erin, you shouldn't go out in this."

"It's fine. I've driven through worse. And the rains aren't bad enough to flood anything yet," she said. "I'll be back in a few minutes."

With a reluctant nod and a sigh, Zach said, "I know better than to think I can stop you once your mind is made up. Just be careful."

Main Street was dark and empty. No cars parked along the road. No lights on in shops as people closed up for the night. Not even the street lamps were on. Power must have gone out during the drive over there.

Samantha parked in front of the station and struggled to close the door against a gust of wind whipping from the opposite direction. She braced herself and fought her way to the station door. Once inside, she followed the bright glow of an LED lantern coming from Chief Vidrine's office.

She felt like a moth being drawn in. Only it wasn't the light she was drawn to. It was the promise of solving this case.

And the fear of what she suspected to be true.

"Samantha?"

"It's me," she said.

He gestured for her to sit once she entered the office. "You didn't have to come out here. I don't want to put you in harm's way when we could have discussed this over the phone."

"No, we couldn't," she said. "I was at Erin's. The Sonnier house."

"Oh."

Her cheeks flushed with his sheepish reaction, but she wasn't embarrassed. Erin had been wrong about that much.

After too many years of holding back, Samantha was no longer interested in hiding who she was.

She only hated this uncomfortable disclosure step. She knew Gary would be on her side, but that didn't mean his discomfort as he processed the information didn't make her a little squirmy.

"Sorry," he said. "I didn't realize you two had grown... close."

She nodded. "But she's been through enough. I don't want to involve her in this case any more than she already is."

A knot formed in Samantha's stomach, remembering

how much of the case they'd discussed earlier that evening. She should have never revealed that much and just kept her mouth shut. Erin was already hell-bent on finding out who killed Paul. More information was only going to fuel that flame and could put Erin in danger.

Gary smirked. "Hard to keep that one out of trouble still, I guess."

Samantha felt a sudden tug to defend Erin, but she quickly realized she didn't need to. It was a statement meant with genuine affection, as proven by Gary's warm smile.

"I think we have a problem."

Gary raised his brow. "Yes, I believe we have some missing evidence."

"The bigger problem is who I think may have taken it."

"And who might that be?"

"After Dustin collected the prescriptions from the Sonnier house, Connie remembered seeing them on my desk the next morning. Before the funeral."

"Right," Gary said.

"You were in a meeting when I left." She paused, allowing him to retrace the memories. "With Deputy Fonseca."

Gary thought for a moment, then his eyes widened as his expression fell and his brain put the pieces together.

"Did he leave with anything?" Samantha asked. "Did you see him leave the building?"

"No." Gary's mouth pressed together, then he said with certainty, "I walked out with him. Connie left for the funeral. We stood out front a moment, then he left. He wasn't carrying anything with him. I'm sure of it."

Samantha's shoulders relaxed with the relief that she wouldn't have to arrest a deputy sheriff. At least not for this particular bit of obstruction.

But her stomach rolled as her anxiety cranked up. The feint worry she'd been ignoring roared to the surface with a vengeance. "Was Dustin still here when you left?"

"Yes. He was finishing up a report for me. He was supposed to lock up before he left for the funeral." Gary's brow furrowed even deeper. "Do you think he forgot to lock the door and someone stole the evidence while we were all at the funeral?"

She couldn't blame Gary for not seeing the obvious answer right in front of him. She hadn't wanted to see it either. But it was the only answer, and she couldn't ignore it. No matter how outrageous or painful it sounded.

"No, I think he locked up before he left."

"Well then, how..." His voice trailed off as her implication hit him with full force. "You can't possibly think—"

"I don't want to think it. But I can't see any way that evidence walked off my desk."

"We can't jump to conclusions here."

"No, we can't." She stood and made a beeline for Dustin's desk.

Gary was only a step behind her. "Maybe he misplaced them and forgot where he left them."

Samantha opened the bottom drawer of his desk,

lifted a stack of files, and held up a plastic bag like it was a prize-winning redfish. "Misplaced them in the bottom of his desk drawer?"

The door rattled in protest against a powerful gust of wind while Gary stood frozen, staring at the bag in Samantha's hand. His jaw was slack, hanging with the weight of disbelief.

Samantha hadn't wanted to believe it either. She'd wanted more than anything to be wrong. But she was holding the proof.

Dustin had taken the prescriptions from Erin's house. He'd hidden evidence in a murder investigation. The only questions now to be answered were why and who he was working with. Samantha didn't believe for a second that Dustin was involved in this alone.

"I think I need to sit down." Gary eased himself into the nearest chair beside Samantha's desk, his eyes still focused on the bag in her hand.

"How should we handle this?"

Gary shook his head. "I don't know. I...I can't believe it."

"We should put these someplace safe now. In your office? Do you have somewhere we can lock it up?"

Dustin or someone else would be back for the evidence once he realized it was missing. For real this time.

After a deep breath, Gary stood and held out his hand. "I have a filing cabinet with a key. I don't trust them in parish evidence. Not yet."

Samantha nodded and handed over the evidence.

Until they knew what was going on and how deep this went, they needed to be careful and keep their investigation contained.

Gary disappeared into his office and returned a few moments later. "Locked up. Key's with me. And I'll keep my office locked too when I'm not around."

He was going through the motions, doing the correct steps, but Samantha could tell he was still in shock. Not just that someone in their own department would do something like this, but *Dustin* of all people.

She needed a reason. Answers. Someone else to blame.

Samantha pulled out the stack of files from his drawer, the ones that had been masking the evidence, and began flipping through them. There had to be something in here. Something that hinted at an explanation for Dustin's connection to a murder. Something that could tell her why and who he'd gotten mixed up with.

The usual list of suspects ran through her head.

Jordan.

Not off the hook entirely yet, although it was clear now that he wasn't the evidence thief.

Randy.

It was no secret he had a pill problem and more than his fair share of run-ins with the law, but her cousin was a reckless criminal. This was too well-planned for him. He would have made a mistake or run his mouth and gotten caught by now.

The doctor.

They had as much at stake as anyone, maybe more,

but murder? That seemed a stretch. These kinds of people tended to flee in the middle of the night and set up shop in a different town.

Nathan.

Everything always came back to Nathan. A man who was used to getting what he wanted. A man who had a business and a reputation and expensive habits to uphold.

Had he finally met his match in Michael Sonnier? The one person who would never take a payoff and had a moral compass stronger than anyone you'd ever meet?

The room spun as she suddenly realized they might have missed something.

What if Paul hadn't been the only victim? What if they'd rushed to assume Mr. Sonnier died of natural causes because he was an old man with no known enemies? His medical records had shown he suffered from mild arrhythmia, so no one had suspected anything might have caused that cardiac failure other than Father Time.

Samantha's heart pounded against her rib cage.

She had to find something tying Nathan to Dustin. Something solid. Something he couldn't weasel out of this time. If they didn't have irrefutable evidence, he'd make this entire investigation look like she was just a vengeful, unhinged ex-wife.

Samantha vowed to find the evidence they needed and hand it over to Gary. This wasn't about proving herself to anyone or about the election. It wasn't about making Nathan pay for what he'd done to her.

This was about getting justice for Paul. And maybe Michael Sonnier as well.

Inside a file folder, she found a paper from the parish lab. The initial toxicology report on Paul.

"When did this get in?"

Gary's brow furrowed. "I didn't know it had."

She checked the date. "Looks like it was just filed yesterday. That was fast."

But why hadn't Dustin shown it to either of them?

Probably the same reason he had a bag full of evidence in his desk drawer.

She looked over the lab results while Gary peered over her shoulder. Not much to look at. The right amount of oxycodone for a man with a lingering injury and a painkiller addiction, and not much else.

"Well, I'll be damned," said Gary.

Samantha squinted at the other item on the report: pentobarbital. "What's that?"

"Did Paul have seizures?"

"Not that I know of," Samantha replied. "No one close to him mentioned it."

"My mama was epileptic and was on that for a while," he said. "I don't remember for sure, but that seems like a lot."

"Someone gave Paul seizure meds?"

Her brain raced back to Nathan. The man who'd have easy access to something like that.

Gary frowned and grunted. "I remember researching the stuff. That isn't all it's used for."

Samantha's stomach sank. She had a sickening feeling she wouldn't like what came next. "What else?"

"Euthanasia. For pets."

So Nathan wouldn't be the only person with access to this stuff. A vet's office would be even more likely than a pharmacy to have it in an injectable form.

No.

No, no, no.

Samantha dropped the file and grabbed her phone. No signal.

"Dang it."

She rushed toward the door.

"Samantha, wait. We'll bring them in for questioning after the storm."

"I don't think this can wait."

"At least wait for the eye!" he shouted at her back.

But it was too late.

Samantha was already headed back into the storm.

Chapter Twenty-Four

"YOU DID NOT JUST DRIVE HERE in a hurricane."

Trey stood in the doorway with a flashlight in hand as he frowned at her rain-and-wind-matted hair and pajamas. She hadn't even realized she was wearing her knit pants with the llamas on them when she'd run out of the house.

"Technically, it's only a tiny hurricane at the coast," she said with all the confidence of a weather forecaster. "These are just tropical storm wind bands."

Once the eyewall got closer, that would be another story. But she planned to be out of here and back home again before then.

He narrowed his eyes, unamused by the technicality. "You really do have a death wish, don't you?"

"Nope, not even a little bit," she said. "That's why I'm here. You were telling me who hates me enough to slash my tires. I figure knowing who has it out for me could keep me alive longer."

"I don't know if that was urgent enough information for a trip out in this storm." He stepped aside and held the door open, catching it with both hands as a gust threatened to slam it against the wall. "Hurry up and get inside, before my mom comes out here."

"Ooh, I want to meet your mom. And your dad, too. Unless they'll hate me." Erin chuckled nervously as she stepped inside the dark house. She was picking up on Trey's storm anxiety, and her speech pacing was showing it. "Never mind. Everyone hates me. But I'm used to it. Can I meet them?"

"One, they're both reading in the bedroom, and I'm not bothering them. Two, not everyone hates you. And three, no, you don't want to meet them." He closed the door behind her. "If Mom catches you out in this storm, she won't let you leave until it passes. I have half a mind to do the same."

Erin wiped her wet bangs from her face. "I'll run home as soon as you finish telling me who you saw."

He frowned again. "If I tell you, you have to promise to go back home. Immediately. Before this hurricane or storm or whatever gets any worse."

"Fine," she said. "I promise. Just tell me who it was that you saw by my car that day."

Trey hesitated, then said, "Dustin."

"Dustin? As in Dustin the cop? That Dustin?"

"That's the one," Trey said.

"Well, the station's near where I parked." She

228

remembered Samantha walking to her car and going back to work nearby. "If I parked near a police station, it would make sense there would be cops around."

"Around," Trey said. "Not standing beside your car and looking around. At the time, I thought maybe he got a new car. That's how close he was to it."

It didn't make any sense. Sure, she had a bad track record around here, and she never met a cop who wasn't suspicious of her, but why would Samantha's coworker slash her tire?

Erin didn't even know the guy. He was a couple of years younger than her, and she'd only met him for the first time when he'd come to the house to collect those prescriptions as evidence.

Then Erin remembered what Samantha had said before she'd left.

The chief needs help finding something.

Were the prescriptions missing?

If Dustin lost them, then maybe Samantha wasn't protecting her ex *or* her cousin. Maybe she couldn't tell Erin what was going on because it involved another cop.

Whether she was protecting him or just trying to keep everything above board until they figured out what was going on, it still didn't make sense.

"Why would he slash my tire?"

Even if the guy was involved in covering up the murder or something, what did that have to do with her?

"To stall you?" Trey asked. "Where were you going after that?"

"Nowhere." Erin thought back to Friday. Three days

229

felt like a lifetime ago. "Home. I was on my way back home."

Trey's expression was grim. "So he wanted to stall you. Who else had access to your house, Erin?"

"Just Zach." Erin shook her head. "You can't be suggesting he had something to do with any of this. Why would Zach not want me home?"

"I don't know. Same thing everyone else was looking for?"

The prescriptions. Could Zach have been involved with that somehow?

"No," she said adamantly. "He was at work. I had to wait for him to get off so he could give me a ride home."

Trey only raised an eyebrow in silence.

"Don't look at me like that."

But the thought was in her head now. She didn't know how or why, but it was possible, she supposed. Zach had said he and Dustin graduated together. He'd introduced her to Dustin when he came for the evidence.

But that was a long way from whatever Trey was hinting at here.

"He *said* he was at work," Trey added. "Do you know that for sure? Or could Dustin have been helping him by stalling you?"

"To look for the prescriptions himself? Why?"

"I don't know." Trey's face was tight.

"What aren't you telling me?"

"I don't know anything," he said. "But I heard some stuff a while back. It wasn't a big deal, but now that we're talking about Dustin, I can't get it out of my mind."

Erin took a step backward and leaned against the wall for support. Whatever he was about to tell her, she had a feeling she wouldn't like it. "Spill it."

"You know how Zach has a record?"

"Yeah, but it was some minor bullshit drug possession years ago. He and some friends were in a bar fight in New Orleans, and he got busted with weed. That doesn't make him some criminal mastermind or whatever you're insinuating."

"No, it doesn't. I think the arrest was bullshit, and the drugs don't matter," Trey said. "But the word around here was it wasn't all his. He took the rap for Dustin because Dustin couldn't be a cop with a record. So Zach insisted it was all his."

"Zach's a good friend. That's hardly a crime." Quite the opposite. In fact, it went along with everything she already knew about him. He was kind and loyal. Of course, he'd have his friend's back.

"I'm just saying Dustin owed him."

Erin ran all the information in her head. Connected the dots. Put together the ridiculous theory Trey was implying. "Are you trying to tell me you think Dustin slashed my tire because Zach asked him to? To stall me so he could try to find those prescriptions himself?"

None of this made sense.

And yet, so far, it was the only thing that did make sense. Logically, at least.

"That's exactly what I'm trying to tell you."

Trey's voice was calm and even. This wasn't some

wild, excited half-baked theory. He'd thought this through. He'd considered carefully whether to tell her.

"Why?"

Trey shrugged. "That I don't know."

She blinked at him in silence. Processing. Debating.

"Is your cell signal out, too?"

"Yeah. But Mom and Dad have a landline. I think it's still working."

"Good," she said. "Call Sam at the station. Tell her what you told me. If she's already gone, tell the chief."

"Wait, why don't you call and tell her yourself? You can use our phone."

"I need to get back to the house."

She didn't know what to make of this information and didn't want to believe Zach was involved in any of this, but she knew she needed to get back to the house.

If Trey was even close to being on the right track, even if it was all a misunderstanding and just looked bad, it would be better if Zach wasn't there alone.

And even better if Erin got back there before Samantha returned.

Sam.

Erin wished more than anything that Samantha had been there at that moment to talk all of this out with her. They worked so well together, bouncing ideas and theories off of each other. Like they could ride the same brainwaves together. It was one of the things Erin had really grown to love about whatever was between them.

Or whatever was there before she'd made a mess of it with wild accusations.

Erin would just have to make sense of this on her own. Or at least figure out her next step on her own. And that next step was definitely getting back to the house.

Maybe Samantha would get there shortly after. They could all figure this out together. Erin and Samantha and Zach. He could explain everything to them both. Because there *had* to be an explanation.

"You shouldn't go alone." Trey reached for the phone on a nearby table. "Let's make the call, then go together."

But Erin was already out the door and halfway to her car.

With the rain beating down on her and the wind threatening to knock her off her feet, she shouted over her shoulder, "Just call the station!"

Chapter Twenty-Five

SAMANTHA PARKED between Zach's truck and the empty space where Erin's car had been earlier that evening.

Where Erin's car *should* have been.

The town was under a curfew for the night to give the storm time to pass and for work crews to clear the roads of debris and any downed power lines.

But a curfew had never stopped Erin before, so Samantha didn't know why she'd expected it to this time.

She stared at the blue house with no light shining from the decorative glass panes near the top of the front door. The power must be out on this end of town, too.

A particularly nasty gust shook her car. She waited for it to ease up with her hand on the door handle while the rain whipped sideways against her window. With a brief break in the wind, she pushed open the car door and ran up the steps onto the porch.

She lifted her hand to knock but stopped short.

The point of coming back here had been to talk to Erin. To potentially warn her.

But Erin wasn't here.

Samantha needed a new plan.

Where was Erin, anyway? She'd made a big deal out of Samantha not leaving in the middle of the storm. So why was she driving around town in it now?

She checked her phone for messages again, but she still didn't have a signal.

Not that Samantha expected a message. Erin had been pretty upset when Samantha had left.

Maybe Erin had gone to settle things with her at the station. Any conversation they needed to have could have waited, but Erin wasn't exactly the waiting type. Something Samantha was growing to love about her.

Love?

Samantha decided to process that later.

Erin never made it to the station, and Samantha hadn't passed her on the road.

A gust that had to be near fifty miles an hour almost swept Samantha off the porch.

Erin must have gone somewhere else. But where? And why? What was so important that she'd left during the worst part of this storm?

Zach would know.

Whatever his potential involvement was in the case, they both wanted Erin safe.

Samantha knocked on the door but heard nothing from within. She tested the knob and found it unlocked.

Inside, the house was lit only by a small LED lantern on the living room carpet.

"McFly! McFly! McFlyyyyyyyyy!"

Samantha nearly jumped out of her skin with the bird's screeching.

"Shhh," she urged.

Marty gave a staccato squawk in reply and bobbed his head at her.

A quick glance in the kitchen revealed that Zach wasn't scrounging for more snacks. A puzzle sat unopened on the table.

Samantha made her way down the hall. With every step, her stomach muscles tensed a little more, and she reached a hand to her side, placing it against the service pistol tucked in its holster. She always kept it on her when she was on call, but she never thought she'd need it here tonight.

How did she get here? Creeping through Erin's house in the dark in the middle of a storm, looking for Zach, and reaching for her gun?

She left it at her waist, not wanting to alert him she had any suspicions. Just in case those suspicions were well-founded.

She considered calling out for him, but she decided against it and continued on to Mr. Sonnier's old bedroom. Her bedroom for the night.

The door was closed, the way she'd left it. She pressed her ear to the wood but didn't hear anything from inside. Not even Dexter.

No surprise. He was either sleeping in his little dog

bed or hiding from the storm under the big bed. No cause for alarm.

Samantha turned the knob and opened the door slowly as she tiptoed inside.

She shut the door behind her, so as not to be startled if Zach did wander in from the bathroom or some other innocent task. Then her gaze fell on the outline of the bookshelves.

Samantha crossed the room carefully, feeling her way around the bed and squinting, desperately trying to see in the pitch-black room. When she reached the shelves, a chill went up her spine as her fear and suspicions were now fully realized.

Her fingers felt along the wooden shelves and book spines and the uncharacteristic space between them.

These were not the neatly arranged volumes she'd witnessed previously. Someone had removed books from the shelves. With a quick sweep of her foot, she confirmed books littered the floor.

A high-pitched bark rang out from under the bed behind her.

Dexter.

Before Samantha could reach for her gun, she felt a tug at her waist as it was pulled from the holster. A second later, the barrel pressed against the base of her skull.

"Hey, Sam." The familiar voice spoke her name with a friendly cheer as if they were making lunch plans. "I'd hoped you'd stay at the station."

Samantha put her hands up slowly.

No sudden movements. Nothing to set him off.

"Hey, Zach. Why don't you put the gun down, and we can figure out how to get you out of whatever's going on?"

"Don't think so."

But she felt the barrel pull away from her head, and a small flashlight clicked on, illuminating the bedroom. He shifted so she could see the gun now aimed at her face.

"How about instead, you lock that dog in the bathroom? Nice and easy."

"Zach, we can fix—"

"Now, Sam."

His voice was cold, and his words were measured and steady. This wasn't some innocent guy who'd tripped backward into this. These were the words and the voice of someone who'd thought long and hard and was solid in his decisions.

"Okay, okay," she said. "I'm going to bend down to call him out."

"Really don't want to have to shoot you."

"I know you don't," she said, although she was becoming more unsure of that fact by the second. "I'm not going to give you a reason to."

She crouched beside the bed and called Dexter's name. He responded with a whimper at first, and Samantha couldn't tell if he was scared of the storm or if he'd already had a run-in with Zach before she got there. A quick glance at a small bloodstain on Zach's jean hem told her it was the latter.

It took three calls before he scooted out from beneath

the bed and into Sam's waiting arms. She stood with the dog and made eye contact with Zach. Eye contact reminded people who they were about to shoot. It gave them a conscience check.

But the man staring back at her had already checked his conscience. She was wasting her time.

"Bathroom." He waved the gun at the other end of the room. "Remember, I don't *want* to shoot you."

The bigger problem here was that Samantha didn't know exactly what he did want. And if she didn't know that, she couldn't use the information to her advantage.

Hell, she didn't even know who this guy was anymore.

She carried Dexter into the bathroom with Zach a step behind her, placed the dog on the linoleum, and closed the door with him safely inside.

Still facing the door with her hands in the air again, Samantha said, "Okay, we can—"

A sharp blow hit the side of her head, and the room went black.

Chapter Twenty-Six

ERIN'S whole body relaxed once she saw Sam's Honda parked in front of the house.

She'd been a mess of nerves driving back from Trey's house. Rain had filled the ditches and water began to spill onto the roads, and the winds had picked up to the point where even Erin had to admit being out there was dangerous.

But she made it home just as the winds died down temporarily once the eye passed over, and her body relaxed a little at the sight of that parked car.

Samantha was safe. She was here. They could work out anything else together.

Even what she'd learned from Trey.

Maybe it was nothing. Maybe Trey was wrong. She'd done a good job on the ride over of convincing herself that was the strongest possibility while she dodged stray cane stalks and tree branches.

"Hey, guys! I'm back!"

Erin shut the door behind her. It closed easily now that the eye was over them, and the wind and rain had both come to a halt. For now, at least.

"McFlyyyyy!"

"We're in the kitchen." Zach's voice rang out through the house.

Erin felt a surge of joy as she followed the lantern light into the kitchen.

Zach and Erin were both here waiting for her. Probably making that monstrous puzzle together.

A week ago, she didn't think she could be happy about *anything* in this town or this house ever again. But here she was, joyous over puzzle-making in a hurricane with two people she cared deeply for.

Whatever Zach's involvement with Dustin was, they'd figure it out. Samantha would help him if she could. They were all friends now, and that's what friends did, right? They helped each other when they were in trouble.

But the rainbows and kittens in her head all vanished the moment she stepped into the kitchen.

Zach stood behind Samantha who was slumped forward in one of the dining chairs. The puzzle was still in its box on the table in front of them.

He dangled a gun over Samantha's shoulder and nodded to the chair across the table. "Have a seat. Join us."

Erin blinked hard, over and over, trying to process the scene.

Zach: with a gun.

Samantha: clearly unconscious.

Where did Zach even get a gun? Or was that Sam's?

Panic surged through her as she realized she didn't have the slightest idea if Zach had a gun of his own.

"Sit," he insisted. "*Now.*"

"Marty! Marty! Marty! McFlyyyyyy!"

"Fucking bird," he muttered.

Marty.

Erin had grown used to him. Almost fond of him. Most of the time he was super chill and made adorable chirping noises and sang and did his version of carrying on a conversation. Maybe not curing depression like that study said, but Erin could see why Grandpa had loved him so much. He filled the house with cheer. Except when they had visitors.

No, that wasn't entirely true. He'd been pleasant when Samantha arrived earlier.

Erin had thought the bird hated cops as much as she did, but that wasn't the connection. He was pissed off and screechy every time Zach was around.

She sat as commanded, but glared across the table. "Did you hurt that bird?"

"I never touched that thing if I could help it."

"Well, he hates you. Why is that?"

"He's a bird? He's been pissed off and hating everyone since that old man died."

"No, he—"

Erin stopped short.

He's been pissed off and hating everyone since that old man died.

No. That wasn't true. He hated Zach.

Erin's chest and throat tightened with the truth taking shape within her.

She had to be wrong. Grandpa's death had been from natural causes. Right?

Since she didn't come home after he died, she never heard from anyone directly on that. She'd never pressed for an autopsy. There'd been no need to. He was old. He didn't have any enemies, and he didn't have anything valuable besides the house and Marty and his collectibles, which weren't worth much to anyone but him.

Or so they'd all thought.

"You killed him."

It came out in a whisper.

Everything came out of Erin loud and blunt. It was who she was and everyone around her had to get used to it or get out of the way.

But this particular truth was hard to breathe life into. She didn't want them to be true words. Didn't want them spoken. They slipped out of her mouth anyway.

Zach rolled his eyes and shook the gun beside Sam's head. "Of course, I did. It's why we're all here, right?"

"No." The words came out louder now, and she pushed each one out with the rage simmering in her gut, threatening to boil over. "You killed *Grandpa*."

Zach at least had the decency to allow a brief flash of guilt to reach his eyes. But he quickly blinked it away. "Man was old. People die, Erin. You should know that."

She flinched. It wasn't the statement itself that

stung. The knowledge that anyone she loved could be taken from her at any moment was a fact she learned early on and clutched like a blanket of certainty. She didn't need a reminder from him.

But that *he,* of all people, was trying to weaponize that fact against her right now cut deep.

"So if I have the coroner take another look at the body, they won't find anything unusual. No strange marks? No injection points?"

He stared at her blankly. "You won't be doing anything like that."

"Are you going to kill me, too? Me and Sam? Everyone knows you were here with us. A whole lot of bodies piling up around you would look pretty suspicious." She forcibly relaxed the muscles in her face, trying to give the appearance of concern. "If we figured this out, other people will eventually."

He aimed the gun at her now and shouted, "Think I don't know that?"

"Then how are you going to get out of this, Zach? What's the plan? I don't even understand why you did all of this."

"It's not brain surgery, Erin."

"Money?"

"Bingo."

She thought back to the cash on the bookshelf. "But Grandpa didn't have any. We found his stash. He didn't have enough money to *kill him* for."

"Not his money," Zach said. "He was getting in the way. Should have minded his own business."

"The pills. You were in on it."

"I just told people where they could get their pills easy. All I had to do was go to clubs around New Orleans, talk to people, and get paid. Easy money. Hell of a lot more than I get cleaning from surgeries and picking up literal shit at work. Wouldn't you jump on that? Money like that's a ticket out of here. You of all people aren't gonna judge me for cashing in my ticket."

No, she wouldn't judge him for that part. "That's a long way from murder."

"Like I said, should have minded his own business. And Paul shouldn't have gotten greedy. Could have gotten what he wanted from the doc, but he thought he was gonna scoop up a free stash in here."

"He walked in on you."

"No." Zach looked offended. "Asked me to let him in the place. With you back in town, he wanted to grab whatever was here before you cleared it out. Offered *me* a cut of whatever pills we found. Was running his mouth about seeing your grandpa at the doctor and never at the pharmacy, but the idiot didn't put together that meant there weren't any pills. We had to shut him up."

She didn't miss that *we*.

"This is too much," she said.

"What's too much is living in this dead-end town. Even more too much was doing odd jobs around this place and taking care of that old man for *nothing* while *you* were off living it up in New Orleans." Venom dripped from his words. "Don't pretend like you cared about him now. Be smart, Erin."

She ignored the bait about not caring. "Be smart how?"

"Help me find his notes."

"His notes?"

Erin caught a slight wobble of Sam's head and the tiniest flutter of her eyelashes. Samantha was waking up. But her body remained slumped forward. Whether she was struggling to gain consciousness or pretending to still be knocked out Erin couldn't tell.

"He wrote down *everything*. What he ate every day. Where he bought every God-awful piece of crap in this place. Hell, the man even wrote the date he got *junk mail* on each envelope. You know he kept records. I need them." He smiled, but there was no lightness in his eyes. "And you're gonna find them for me."

"Why would I do that?"

She already knew the answer. Her why was sitting in front of her with a gun aimed at her head.

Erin needed to keep him talking. She needed time to figure out a plan.

But Zach didn't go for the easy why. Not the easy why for Erin, at least. He reached for his own why.

"Because I don't want to kill you, Erin. I like you, believe it or not. And I know you hate this town as much as I do, so I'm gonna offer you a way out. For good. Help me find *everything*, and I'll cut you in on my share. Consider it an advance on the house sale. You can leave this place behind forever."

He did know her. Better than just about anyone.

But he knew the Erin from a week ago. Years ago.

Today's Erin?

She'd kind of grown to like this place. And she wasn't so easily bought off. Especially not by a guy who had killed her grandfather and was now threatening someone else she loved.

Loved.

That was a problem for future Erin to figure out. Present Erin had enough to deal with.

She wasn't about to sit by and let Zach take away someone else that she cared about. Not without a fight.

"What about her?" Erin asked. "She's not going to just let you walk away from this."

"Let me worry about Sam."

"I'm not going along with any plan that involves you killing her."

"Don't want to kill her either. Play nice, and I won't have to."

"Zach, she likes you, but you know Sam has a moral compass the size of Texas."

"I said I won't kill her if you give me what I want. She'll be someone else's problem."

Someone else. There's that *we* again.

"Who?"

"Not information you need to find those records." He waved the gun to the side. "Start in the kitchen. Find whatever crazy-ass hiding places he had like those books, and find his notes." He aimed the gun back at Sam's head. "And nothing funny, Erin. Said I don't want to shoot her. Didn't say I wouldn't."

A chill ran through her body. She might have been

247

doubting everything she knew about Zach, but she didn't doubt a word of what he said at that moment.

With her eyes on Samantha, Erin stood and nodded. "Okay. Let's find those notes."

Chapter Twenty-Seven

SAMANTHA LISTENED CAREFULLY as Erin rummaged through cabinets and drawers only feet away in the tiny kitchen.

"Looked there already. You're supposed to know where he kept stuff."

There was a long pause and Samantha didn't dare a glance, even though she desperately needed to know how he was filling that silence.

Footsteps.

"No clues. No cash. And say bye-bye to Sam."

Crap. He was using her as leverage against Erin. Samantha was supposed to be the one helping Erin. Instead, she'd made herself a liability.

She squeezed her eyes tighter, trying to blink away the pain radiating from the back of her skull.

With her head still slumped forward, pretending to remain knocked out, she squashed her guilt and retraced the last things she remembered.

Putting Dexter in the bathroom.

Zach aiming the gun at her and ordering her to put the dog in there.

Zach telling her to get the dog.

Zach telling her not to move.

Zach's voice in the dark.

The barrel of that gun pressed against her head.

The books.

The books.

He was looking for something. Something Mr. Sonnier hid in this house. More prescriptions maybe? Proof of his involvement?

Samantha wasn't even sure the extent of his involvement yet. All she knew was that he and Dustin were connected to this somehow. Dustin hid the evidence. Zach had access to the house. He'd probably been looking around here for weeks before Erin returned.

Samantha shouldn't have just walked into a trap like that. She should have known better. Should have done better. Been better.

No. That was her mother's voice in her head.

Samantha hadn't wanted to tip him off. She had no way of knowing he'd turn on her so quickly. So violently.

All of her evidence so far had told her she'd most likely find him back in the kitchen making snacks. She'd assumed he'd just gotten in over his head. Gotten paid to find or help hide evidence.

And now she knew who killed Paul.

It had been the one piece of the puzzle she'd been looking for. The missing corner piece that held everything together. Because she always knew Nathan didn't have it in him to get his own hands dirty. But Zach—this Zach—clearly did.

Plus, Zach was a vet tech with access to the drug that killed Paul, and he knew how to use a syringe. Where to place it. How to administer it quickly and efficiently before his patient or victim had a chance to realize what was happening and struggle. He had the means and opportunity since he was the caretaker here.

Motive in this case was irrelevant. Probably money. It was always money around here. Money meant leverage. Or escape. Either way, Zach was obviously her missing corner piece.

Now she just had to take him down.

"Listen," Erin said. "I told you. He had a million different places where he kept things. And he rearranged his system all the time. I don't know if he was bored or paranoid, but apparently, he had good reason to be paranoid."

"Erin." Zach's voice was cold and insistent.

Samantha wanted to fly across the room and strangle him for the implied threat in just Erin's name.

"I'm looking, I'm looking."

Erin probably didn't know where Mr. Sonnier kept whatever Zach was looking for, but Samantha had no doubt that she was stalling. Erin was clever and strategic, and she knew exactly how far to push Zach before he snapped.

Or, at least, she thought she knew.

Samantha needed to help. She wiggled her hands to

assess the binding on her wrists. Secure. No surprise there. A boy scout he might not be, but Zach was handy.

What he didn't know was to make sure his victim's hands were in the proper position before securing them. He'd bound her hands behind the chair but with her wrists side by side. Rookie move.

While Erin rummaged noisily through the pantry mumbling about some anecdote from her childhood, Samantha turned her arms inward, maneuvering her wrists to face each other and loosening the hold of those zip ties Zach had probably found in a junk drawer.

"Enough." Zach walked over to Samantha and bent so she could feel his breath against her ear and cheek. No doubt checking that she was still passed out. He stepped away and said, "Next room. Move."

Samantha held her breath, listening as two sets of footsteps exited the kitchen. A moment later, they were out of the room, and she could hear Erin talking at Zach from the bedroom, intentionally loud enough for Samantha to know where they were. Samantha shimmied her hands up and out of the ties and flew to her feet, tiptoeing swiftly toward the hallway.

"Been through every book in this place now that I know about that shit. And every piece of *collectible crap* before that for the last few weeks."

His words oozed with disgust as Samantha padded down the hall, using the darkness as a shield.

"Must be other hiding spots. Where, Erin? Where would he keep his most important information? I've been through this whole place. Must have some kind of secret hiding spot. A loose floorboard. A false drawer I missed. *Something*."

There was a desperation beneath his voice that Samantha hid missed before. Or maybe the fear was just now surfacing. Who had he promised this information to? What was he afraid of if he didn't deliver?

Nathan.

It had to be.

But that didn't matter right now. Zach was still determined enough and deranged enough that she couldn't imagine talking him out of whatever his mission was. If Erin hadn't been able to do it, no one else stood a chance.

"Do you think he showed *me* his super secret hiding spot? I wasn't exactly the most reliable kid, Zach. You know that."

A floorboard creaked.

"If you can't help find it, why am I keeping you alive?"

Every cell in Samantha's body wanted to launch her into the room and tackle him. But he had a gun and Erin, and with her wooziness from the blow to her head, she wasn't sure she could move quickly enough to disarm him from this distance before he got a shot off.

"Because you don't want to shoot me? Remember?" Erin's signature hubris and charm were on full display, her voice carrying the weight of ten good hostage negotiators. She knew what Zach wanted and was using it to her advantage. "And two pairs of eyes are better than one."

"Just hurry up. Wouldn't wanna have to explain to Sam why you've made a return to your life of crime."

Samantha couldn't imagine how betrayed Erin must be feeling right now. Zach had been her only friend when she'd come back to town. He'd been helping her. He'd cared for her grandfather.

And possibly killed him.

She ignored her latest suspicion for now. They could worry about adding to Zach's list of charges later.

Samantha crept toward the doorway. They were on the other side of the bed, but if she was fast, she could probably reach him before he realized she was there.

Her best guess was that he'd use Erin as a shield.

She couldn't let that happen. This was too big a gamble.

Erin pointed at the wooden floor. "I'm going to reach down. Okay?"

When he looked where she was pointing, Erin gave a quick shake of her head in Samantha's direction. Samantha could barely spot the subtle signal, but Erin clearly didn't want her to make a move yet. She had a plan.

Samantha didn't like her odds, but Erin taking the initiative and putting herself at risk made her equally nervous.

If she had to choose an option, Samantha would choose trusting in Erin.

Not because she didn't trust herself. She'd come far enough in the last week to shake off most of the damage to her confidence Nathan had done.

She was trusting that Erin knew Zach best. If he had a weakness, Erin would know how to exploit it.

Samantha didn't have anything to prove here. All she had to do was trust in this woman who'd won her heart over the last few days. The person who'd helped her see and trust in herself.

The least she could do to return that favor was trust in Erin and her plan.

Samantha held her ground and gave a quick nod.

Chapter Twenty-Eight

"TICK-TOCK, ERIN."

"I'm going, I'm going." She stared at the floor in front of her and the space between where they stood and the wall. "Just trying to remember which board it was."

"Thought you didn't know where the notes were," Zach said. "No funny shit. Remember—"

"Yeah, yeah, yeah, you don't want to shoot me. I get it." She kept her voice light and sarcastic, squashing her rage. She couldn't believe she hadn't seen this side of Zach before now. How had she missed it? "I still don't know if the notes are here, but I know where he kept some stuff from my parents. Sentimental shit. Maybe he put them there."

That shut Zach up. Maybe he had killed her grandfather, but they did share the same dead-parents-wound.

That wound was his soft spot. Maybe the only one.

It was his weakness.

"Good," he said, somber now. "Let's see if they're in there."

Erin found the loose board and pried it up, revealing an open box her grandfather had cut into and secured beneath the subfloor. She hadn't been lying to Zach. She really had forgotten about this spot until just a few moments ago. And why would she remember? It was filled with things she'd been trying most of her life to forget.

A quick look didn't reveal a notebook. But knowing her grandfather, he would have hidden something like that beneath the more mundane things like her mother's favorite t-shirt folded neatly on top of everything else.

Erin froze. She'd forgotten all about that shirt.

She reached into the box and held up the worn black t-shirt with all four Golden Girls smiling on the front. Erin felt her eyes tearing up and blinked them back as she remembered her mother wearing this shirt every weekend. It was one of the only memories she had of her.

"Cut out the memory lane stuff or move out of the way," an impatient Zach growled behind her.

Erin dropped the t-shirt to the side of the hole and dug a little deeper inside. One hand palmed exactly what she'd been looking for, while the other hand came up with something else.

"I think this might be it."

She really hadn't expected the notes to be in here, but there they were. On a yellow legal pad. Every visit her grandfather took to that pill mill. Dates and times. Records of every call he made to the pharmacy, too.

Along with notes asking about the safety of refilling such heavy doses so soon.

"Let me see."

Erin held the legal pad in her lap, forcing Zach to lean over her shoulder. His attention was captured by that all-caps handwriting on the paper, but he still held the gun behind her.

This was her only chance. Their only chance.

As he leaned down even further and reached for the pad with his free hand, Erin made one swift move, twisting and bringing up the treasure in her other hand to connect with his eye.

Zach screamed out in pain as the metal sank into his eyeball with a sickening squish. Erin dropped her weapon, then spun around to face him, grabbing the gun now dangling loosely from his fingers.

Samantha appeared beside her a second later and grabbed Zach. She held his arms behind his back as he screamed and blood poured down his face.

"Zachary Hebert, you are under arrest for threatening with a firearm, assault, and kidnapping an officer of the law. And a whole bunch of other stuff I'm sure the DA will love to add to the list."

Erin was frozen, still stunned at what she'd just had to do. She felt hot tears of relief spilling down her cheeks.

"You okay?"

Erin nodded. "You?"

"I'll live. Thanks to your quick thinking." Samantha gestured at the bloody metal object on the ground. "What is that?"

Erin didn't want to touch the thing now that it had blood and Zach's eye juice all over it.

"A visor clip. St. Florian. Patron saint of firefighters. Mom bought it for my dad's car to keep him safe." Erin couldn't help the sarcastic chuckle that escaped. "They'd taken my mom's car instead of his on the day of the crash."

Samantha held Zach tight by the arm and gave a sympathetic cringe at that bit of irony. "I'm glad it was in there. Did you know?"

"Not about the notes. But I knew Grandpa kept the clip in here. He'd wanted me to have it when I started driving, but I remembered how pointy those angel wings were and told him I was more likely to be impaled by the thing than saved by it."

Samantha gave a sad but comforting smile. "We should call an ambulance."

Erin forced herself to look at Zach, slumped and held by Samantha. Rage replaced her shock and relief once again. "Okay, but what if—"

"Call the ambulance." It came out as an order that ended in a nervous chuckle of exhaustion. "Grab my handcuffs from the car too, please. Or zip ties if you have more here. I, unlike Zach here, know how to use them properly."

Samantha stood aside while paramedics strapped a patched-up Zach to the gurney and wheeled him out of the bedroom. She'd already handcuffed one of his wrists to the rail, so he wasn't going anywhere.

Marty squawked as they rolled past his cage.

A parish deputy was taking Erin's statement in another room, while Trey sat with her. Apparently, Erin had told Trey to call Samantha at the station, and upon hearing more of the story and not being able to reach Samantha, Chief Vidrine had decided to call in the cavalry.

The storm had been downgraded and the back end of it fell apart as it moved over land, so it was mostly just gusty on the other side of the eye now. Despite the curfew still in effect until dawn, Trey had arrived before the ambulance and the chief and half the sheriff's department. He refused to stay outside and hadn't left Erin's side, which made Samantha feel a little better about being separated from her.

Samantha had enough to deal with, anyway. Jordan insisted on getting the run-down of everything that had happened over the last couple of hours. She'd given him the basics so far, careful not to divulge anything in front of Zachary. Even though he'd been half-conscious due to the pain, they needed to keep a lock on the evidence they had against him.

"I know you're going to file a report, and I know you'll cross and dot everything like you always do," Jordan said. "But Sam, if Dustin really was involved, we can't risk anyone getting off on a technicality or some lawyer spinning a frame-up or cover-up."

Samantha turned to him in shock. Was that a compliment tucked in there? From Jordan?

"My report will be pristine," she promised. "But I'm handing the case over to your department. For exactly those reasons."

Jordan blinked at her. "You fought for this case like a starving tiger, and now you're going to just give it up? I thought I'd have to gladiator brawl you for it."

Samantha didn't care about the glory of solving this case. She never did. She wanted to bring Paul's killer to justice and protect the people in this town, and she'd still have a hand in that. The difference now was she didn't give a damn if handing over the case cost her the election.

She still wanted to be chief, but if she hadn't earned the respect of this town by now, she never would. All she could do was be true to herself and continue to do the next right thing.

Chief Vidrine entered the room, his figure casting a large shadow on the wall from a lantern on the floor. The storm was dying down, but the power was still out and would be until the morning. He shook his head at the blood on the wooden floor and the ice pack Samantha held against the back of her skull.

"Ah good, you're here," Jordan said. "Make sure your sergeant gets checked out before the EMTs leave. I'm pretty sure she has a concussion."

"I probably do," she admitted. "But it's still the right thing to do."

"What's the right thing?" Chief Vidrine asked.

Jordan answered for her. "Sam here is giving the case to me. No fight. Just handing it over."

"No," she corrected. "I said I'm handing the case over to the parish. I think you should recuse yourself as well."

Jordan scoffed. "And why would I do that?"

"Because those notes Erin is giving to the deputy in the other room tie your biggest campaign donor to the investigation."

Jordan's expression fell as she spoke and the words sank in.

"I swear, I didn't—"

"Doesn't matter," Samantha insisted. "Like you said, we don't want anyone getting off on a technicality or claiming police involvement."

It was clear he was putting the pieces together the way she had. As much as he wanted to win and as much as he wanted Nathan's money, Jordan couldn't have his campaign tainted this way. It might already be tanked, but he couldn't afford to look like he was protecting Nathan. That could cost him more than the election.

"We both know Nathan has been bankrolling your campaign," she said.

Chief Vidrine frowned. "She's right. It wouldn't look good for you if he's under investigation while you're running the case. Plus, Zach is gonna save his own behind and sing his head off for a deal first chance he gets."

That was probably also true. Zach couldn't possibly have any loyalty to Nathan or the doctor. And he was smart enough to know that they'd turn on him in a heartbeat if he didn't get his own deal first.

Jordan stood quietly, his mouth pressed tightly as he ran all the facts and scenarios through his head.

Bottom line, whether Jordan knew anything about what was going on, Nathan had screwed him the way he'd screwed everyone else around him.

"Excuse me."

Samantha and Gary stepped aside for Jordan to pass between them and leave the room. Gary gently pulled aside her hand holding the ice pack and examined Samantha's head.

"That looks pretty nasty."

"They already looked at it. I'll be fine. Just need to monitor for worsening symptoms and not be alone for the night."

Gary cleared his throat and put the ice pack back against the lump. "I suppose that last point is taken care of?"

Samantha nodded.

"Good," Gary said. "Well, I'm going to check on things outside. You okay for now?"

"Wait." She hesitated. "Dustin?"

Gary took a deep breath and exhaled. "Jordan's got deputies picking him up for questioning. They have enough to make an arrest, but we're hoping he comes clean first. He's gonna pay the price for everything he's done, but sounds like he got caught in a rolling snowball he didn't see coming. He'll lose his badge for sure, but

I'm more concerned that we get *everyone* involved in this."

She nodded again, and he left her alone. Samantha wanted desperately to let Dexter out of the bathroom, but with all the strangers still running around the house taking statements and collecting evidence, that wasn't a great idea.

Besides, he was safe where he was for now. Once everyone was gone, she could snuggle him the whole rest of the night.

Erin entered the doorway and stopped, waiting for Samantha to spot her before entering. Probably not wanting to startle her after being hit from behind earlier in the night.

Samantha crossed the room and caught Erin in her arms. They held each other tightly, and Erin let out a shuddering release of breath against Sam's shoulder.

They'd barely had time to breathe, much less process all that had happened before people showed up. There was so much Samantha wanted to say. So much she wanted to ask. But her conscience got the first word.

"I'm so, so sorry. I should have put it all together earlier."

Erin pulled back and looked at Samantha in disbelief. "He was my friend. I'm the one who should have figured it out. I'm the one who invited you here and put you in danger."

"Yeah, but we got out of it. Together."

A wide grin stretched across Erin's face. "Yeah, we did." Her grin disappeared. "Is he gone?"

Samantha nodded. "Ambulance took him. A few minutes ago. You'll still have a full house for a while, though. I'll clean this up for you once they're gone and the scene is cleared. Don't worry about it."

Samantha wasn't about to let Erin clean up Zach's blood from her grandfather's bedroom. She'd take care of it as soon as she could, then she'd be able to let Dexter out, too.

"So you're staying?"

"You couldn't get rid of me tonight if you tried."

"Sorry, I kind of did try." Erin took a big, shame-filled breath and exhaled. "Sorry I jumped to conclusions like that."

"It's okay. You didn't have all the information. You had to piece things together with what you had."

"But I should have trusted you."

"Erin, we haven't known each other that long. And you've had enough reasons in your life not to trust people. I get it."

"You came back, though," Erin said. "And you trusted me to handle Zach."

"I did." That had been the hardest part. Trusting someone else to handle the situation and not trying to rush in and take care of it herself. "You did a pretty good job of handling things, by the way."

"Thank you. You did pretty well yourself, sergeant."

Samantha grinned and pulled Erin close again to kiss her. There was a house full of people, but she didn't care who saw them. Didn't care who saw *her*. The real her.

Erin pulled away from the kiss but held her close. "Power will still be out until the morning, right?"

"Right. Crews won't go out for repairs until first light."

"Up for making that puzzle in the dark?"

"I'm not sitting at that table," Samantha said with a chuckle. "Not tonight, at least."

"Fair enough," Erin said. "I'm not playing cards anywhere."

"Also fair." Samantha tightened her grip on Erin and smiled. "I'm sure we'll find something to pass the time."

Chapter Twenty-Nine

"NOPE." Erin took Samantha's face in her palms and turned her away from what had caught her attention. She stared into Samantha's warm brown eyes and wished she could also wrap her arms around her body. But Erin only had two hands, and they already had an assignment. "You told me not to let you look at that thing until it was time."

Samantha's lips stretched into a big, goofy grin. A week ago, Erin wouldn't have thought it was possible for anything to look goofy on Samantha. But as they'd spent more time together and as Samantha had relaxed more around Erin, small quirky expressions began to make appearances. It only made Erin fall even harder for the woman in front of her.

"No, you're right," Samantha said. "Do *not* let me watch the election coverage until the results are in."

"Want me to turn that thing off?" Addie waved her dish towel at the TV behind Samantha's head.

Above the scrolling chyron displaying poll closure times, Nathan Ardoin was being led out of his home in handcuffs. They'd seen it already. Samantha had watched it on repeat with a satisfied smile on her face.

"No, we're fine," Erin said. "But thanks."

"Good, because I wasn't planning on it. Just being polite."

Erin laughed and shook her head as Addie winked and disappeared into the kitchen.

Samantha's mom had already begun planning an election night event in the nearest hotel meeting room. But Samantha told her to cancel it. She would be celebrating somewhere else.

Addie's Lunch Shack was the perfect place to spend election night.

Melanie hurried in and leaned against the counter as she caught her breath beside her sister. When Samantha had introduced them at a press conference a few days ago, Melanie had immediately wrapped Erin in a hug and thanked her for bringing a smile back to her sister's face.

"Did I miss it?"

"Nope," Erin said. "Still waiting."

"Not so patiently," Samantha added. "If I could get this whole night over with, that would be great."

"No," Melanie said. "Basking in the glow of everything you've earned and all the potential good you'll do will be great."

Erin pointed a thumb at Melanie. "Yeah, what she said."

Samantha might be nervous, but Erin had no doubt she would win this thing. And since Addie's had been the place where they'd met—or at least where they'd *re-met* —it was the perfect place to celebrate with all of their friends.

It also made it the perfect place for Erin to break her big news.

She'd gone back and forth about whether to tell Samantha tonight. On the plus side, it would make a good distraction while they waited for the election results. Even if Samantha didn't respond well to Erin's announcement, they'd still have Samantha's victory to lighten the mood. And if the election didn't go the way Samantha wanted, then at least they might have some other good news to celebrate and soften the blow. If Samantha would indeed be happy about what Erin was about to tell her.

Either way, it was a solid plan. But Erin didn't want her news to steal even the tiniest bit of Samantha's thunder, so maybe she should wait.

She was overthinking things.

This town was rubbing off on her already.

Melanie squeezed Samantha's shoulders and excused herself for a bathroom break before the results came in.

"So what was it you wanted to tell me?" Samantha wrinkled her brow. "You were being all cryptic on the way here, and it sounded serious."

"It is. I think. Maybe." Erin took a deep breath and blew it out in a pinpoint stream.

269

"Just tell me." Samantha's voice wavered. "You're going back to New Orleans soon, aren't you?"

Erin hated the sadness in Samantha's voice. Hated how small those words sounded. Samantha, her rock, was terrified.

Good thing she was dead wrong.

"Actually, the opposite," Erin said. "Grandpa's house is officially not for sale."

Samantha straightened her back as her eyes widened. "Are you serious?"

Erin nodded. "Since it's paid off, I won't have to worry about rent like I did in New Orleans, so I can keep selling my jewelry online and maybe even have enough to open a little shop in that empty space downtown."

"A shop? For your jewelry?" Samantha let out a gasp and grabbed both of Erin's hands. "That's so exciting!"

"Not just for me, though. I could open it up to everyone around here who has art or makes stuff. Like, I heard Ms. Pellerin is still painting. And Mr. Robicheaux makes the coolest metalwork creations in his forge. I was thinking they could put their art in there on consignment, or we'd work out some way to sell their stuff, too."

Tears pooled in the rims of Sam's eyes. Tears that were making Erin's eyes water now.

Dang it. She wasn't supposed to cry. This wasn't supposed to be a crying thing.

"That sounds wonderful."

"Then why are you crying." Erin rubbed furiously at her own face.

"Because it makes me so happy that you're staying

here. That you seem happy here now." She paused. "You are happy here now, aren't you? Because you seem—"

"Yes, *yes!* Of course, I'm happy," Erin said. "I'm happier than I've been in… well, as long as I can remember."

Samantha smiled. "Good. I'm really glad."

"And that's the other thing I wanted to tell you."

"Oh? Two things?"

"Yes. Sort of," Erin said. "But related kind of."

"Well, tell me!" Samantha sounded like a kid being asked to wait an extra five minutes for a cookie.

"Okay, okay, jeez." But Erin couldn't be happier. She liked making Samantha wait for news. Especially this news. "If I'm going to be staying here, I want to try things for real."

Samantha raised her brow. "Things?"

"Us. I want to try *us* for real. If you want to." Erin took another deep breath and held it this time. Finally, she took the leap. "Because I love you, Samantha Keller Ardoin."

It had happened so quickly. Erin wasn't used to letting herself feel anything, but she didn't want to fight what she felt for Samantha. Besides, everything else had happened so quickly since she'd been back here. Why not this?

Samantha took a sharp inhale, then relaxed her shoulders and grabbed Erin's face in her palms. She stared directly into Erin's eyes and said, "I love you, too. And I'm so glad you're going to be sticking around so I can show you how much every single day."

271

Samantha pressed her lips to Erin's mouth, and Erin melted against her. Her whole body tingled with the rush of those words and all the promises held within them.

"So I guess that means you told her?"

Erin smiled against Samantha's mouth and gave two small kisses before pulling away.

"Hello, Trey," Samantha said as he took a seat on the barstool beside Erin. "Yes, she did."

"Good." He grinned at the pair of them. "I like those smiles. They look good on both of you."

"Why, thank you." Erin held her arms out wide to pull both of them in close. "Look at us. We're gonna take this town by storm, I tell you."

Trey rolled his eyes but exchanged a gleeful look with Samantha. "As long as you don't call us the Queer-keteers or anything like that."

Erin gasped with her mouth wide open. "That's it! You said it!"

"Nope," Samantha said. "Veto!"

"Wait, we didn't even decide on veto powers or procedures yet!"

"Well, it's two to one, so you're outvoted, anyway." Trey tapped the counter. "Since you're sticking around and we can officially talk about that now, we can discuss that favor you owe me."

After the way Trey had stepped up to make sure Erin was okay that night of the storm when everything went down, she'd agree to anything for him. Even if she hadn't already owed him a favor.

"What'll it be?"

"Can you help design and make something for my mom's birthday next month? I'll pay you, of course. I just want to give her something special, like one-of-a-kind personalized earrings or whatever."

A wide grin made its way to Erin's face. She'd been doing a lot of grinning lately, and her face wasn't quite used to it yet. But around these people, she couldn't help it.

"I'd be honored to make something for her."

"Thanks." Trey pointed at the TV. "Speaking of voting. Looks like I made it here just in time."

Melanie rushed back to the group, and the four of them watched together as the news anchor announced Samantha had won the election. Addie's Lunch Shack erupted in applause, and Addie came around the counter to hug Samantha.

Erin kissed Samantha again, in front of the whole diner full of cheering citizens.

When she pulled away, Erin wiped the tears from Sam's cheeks and kissed her again.

"Congratulations."

"Thanks." Samantha blinked back more tears and said the sweetest words Erin had ever heard, "Welcome home."

Chapter Thirty

SAMANTHA ENTERED the shop space as Erin held the door open for her. Erin's smile was as wide as that doorway, and she had a lightness to her movements that really suited her.

Ever since Erin decided to stay in Etta, Samantha had noticed a change in her. And it wasn't just in the pink streaks she'd put in her hair during a quick trip to settle some things in New Orleans.

"So, what do you think?" Erin bit her lip in an uncharacteristic display of hesitancy.

Samantha barely resisted the urge to forget all about the shop and meet those lips with her own.

She looked around the space. She imagined it just as Erin had described the plans to her during several evenings when Erin had been processing ideas out loud. Samantha had learned quickly that her girlfriend was an external processor.

That is when she utilized any processing time at all.

Samantha cherished those verbal brainstorming sessions. She loved the sound of Erin's voice. The fever and pitch of her idea tornadoes. Her energy was contagious, and Samantha was just glad to be in her orbit to soak it all up whenever she could.

"I think it's going to be fantastic," Samantha said. "You've already got it halfway there."

After the paperwork went through, Erin dove right into setting up the place and making plans. She'd finished painting the walls a couple of days ago and couldn't wait to show Samantha.

"Do you really like it?" Erin bit her lip again. "It's a little brighter in here than the swatches I showed you."

The sun streaming in through the street-facing windows did bring some intensity to the color. But the pale yellow looked even better this way.

Erin had wanted some color in the store, but not too much. Something to add interest, but nothing that would compete with the beautiful items she and her fellow artists and craftspeople would be showcasing.

"I think it's even better than I imagined. Very sunny. Very you."

Erin laughed. "I don't think I've ever been called sunny before."

"That's because you never let people see the real you before." Samantha moved closer and tucked a streak of pink behind Erin's ear. "I'm grateful every day that you let me in."

A shy grin spread across Erin's face. Samantha pulled her close and gave her a quick kiss.

"Seriously, I love it. It's perfect."

"It's not even close to finished," Erin said.

"I know, but your vision is coming through loud and clear every step of the way. I'm so happy for you."

"Thanks. I couldn't have done it without your support."

"I doubt that," Samantha said. "I'm pretty sure you could do just about anything you got your heart set on."

"Maybe. But having you in my corner definitely helps."

Samantha squeezed her hand. "Good."

"Speaking of people in one's corner. You still meeting with Trey's mom after work?"

Samantha's first order of business after she won the election was to reach out to Trey to see if she could chat with his mom sometime. And not about him.

Since Trey's mom worked in healthcare, she had connections to EMS and crisis workers. Samantha wanted to set up a volunteer network of emergency, health, and social workers to take some calls the police department really shouldn't be handling. Cases like Trey's. New Orleans had launched a similar kind of crisis intervention unit, and they were going to discuss what they might be able to implement in more rural areas.

Erin had been right. Samantha couldn't handle everything on her own. Nor should she. Some things were better handled by other more qualified people.

Trey's mom was intrigued by the idea, even if she was a little skeptical at first. But she was willing to discuss potential logistics with Samantha.

The plan was to have the volunteers respond to sensitive calls along with the police for now, and Samantha would work on her end to build a permanent program into the town's budget. Once she was officially police chief, she'd have more say in making something like that a reality.

"Yeah, I am," Samantha said. "Shouldn't be too late, though. Want to come hang out with me and Dexter at my place after?"

They'd been spending a lot of time together over the last few weeks, and they'd realized it was easier with Dexter to have Erin come over at night. Samantha wanted more than anything to ask Erin to move in. Yeah, it was fast, but it felt right.

Samantha didn't want to spook Erin, though. So she held back. For now.

Plus, Erin was reacquainting herself with that house and all of her memories. She needed time to heal.

Samantha would bring it up when the time was right. And she was confident that it would be one day soon.

"Definitely. Text me when you're done." Erin rubbed her hand along Samantha's arm. "I guess I'd better let you get back to work, huh?"

"Unfortunately, yeah."

They'd been swamped at the station since they hadn't hired a replacement for Dustin yet. The former deputy had cut a deal for his cooperation with the investigation, but he would never work in law enforcement again.

At least Dustin had the good sense to take the deal. Nathan would have thrown him under the bus with everyone else in his wake.

As for Jordan, he continued to insist he knew nothing about any of it, and there was no evidence to prove otherwise. Either way, his association with Nathan killed whatever chance he had in the election.

Thankfully, Chief Vidrine was still there until Samantha's term would officially begin next month. He promised to continue helping out as needed, but they'd need another deputy as soon as possible. They had a couple of qualified applicants, but the process for getting someone new in was taking longer than Samantha would have liked.

Erin walked Samantha out and held the door open for her again. "Oh, are we having dinner with your mom this weekend?"

"I still haven't decided."

"You know I've got your back either way, right?"

"You do know what that means?" Samantha laughed. "Dinner with my family is a whole thing. You'd be miserable."

"I'd be with you. I could never be miserable. But if you'd be miserable, we don't have to go."

"I'm not afraid," Samantha said. "Or embarrassed or whatever you might think. I just don't want to put you through that."

Erin shrugged. "I can take it. I'm used to people not liking me. It'll be a fun challenge to see if I can win her over at some point."

"I'm her own daughter and haven't managed that yet."

"We can go or not," Erin said. "But don't avoid it for me. Make the decision for you."

"There's kind of an us now."

"There is," Erin said. "But you need to decide how you want to handle your family first and foremost. For you. Knowing I've got your back the way you've done for me with this place and everything else."

Samantha felt a warmth triggered by those words. A warmth she was coming to expect and welcome.

Erin was right. She did need to figure out her relationship with her mother, especially, and how she wanted her family to fit into her life.

Or maybe it was the other way around. Maybe she needed to go to this dinner with Erin to show them who she was now, and maybe they were the ones who needed to decide if they were going to fit in her life exactly the way it was.

She already knew Melanie's answer. She'd have Samantha and Erin's backs in this for sure.

"Thanks. I love you." She kissed Erin once more, then walked out onto the sidewalk towards the station.

"See you tonight!" Erin called out behind her, loud enough for her new shop neighbors and half of Main Street to hear.

Let them all hear. They all knew about Samantha's relationship by now, anyway, considering how gossip flew in that town.

But it was good for them to know that Erin and

Samantha weren't going to be quiet about it. They were going to be who they were, individually and as a couple. The residents of Etta would have to deal with it. So far, to Samantha's surprise, they were dealing with it just fine. More than fine, in most cases.

Just another surprise in a long list of surprises over the last month. Including the woman waving goodbye who Samantha would see again later that night.

And again the next night.

And every night after that, if she got her way.

Free Novella

A dead guy, a dog, and Susan's ex in her truck.

What else could go wrong?

Take a delivery truck ride through New Orleans in this sapphic second chance romantic mystery.

Get *Out for Delivery* FREE:

https://leighlandryauthor.com/out-for-delivery/

Also by Leigh Landry

NOL SERIES

Collie Jolly

(holiday prequel novella)

Because You Can

Sing the Blues

Here You Go

PARANORMAL SAPPHIC ROMANCE

All My Hexes

BAYOU RESCUE SERIES

Hiss and Make Up

At First Meow

CAJUN TWO-STEP SERIES

Second Fiddle Flirt

Six String Sass

Rim Shot Rebound

Squeeze Box Belle

Complete Cajun Two-Step Box Set

About Leigh Landry

Leigh Landry is a contemporary romance author who loves stories with happy endings, supportive friendships, and adorable pets. Once a musician, freelance writer, and English teacher, Leigh now spends her days writing and volunteering at an animal rescue center in the Heart of Cajun Country.

Printed in Great Britain
by Amazon